Will You Marry Me?

BOOK TWO

The Courtship of Lizzie Andrews

Published by PJ Watters Books LLC
ISBN: 978-0-9908644-2-4

Book design by Nancy Barnes, StoriesToTellBooks.com
Cover design original watercolor by Michaela Slattery
Cover design image of couple source Victorian Picture Library

Image credits:
B & M Railroad at Hamilton, Image courtesy of Wenham Museum, Wenham, MA.

Beadle's Dime Ball-Room Companion and Guide to Dancing, source Library of Congress Music Division, American Memory Dance Instruction Manuals

Claflin-Richards House, Wenham, Massachusetts, Image courtesy of Wenham Museum, Wenham, MA.

Hamilton Hall, historic building, est. 1805 source Fletcher6 file from Wikimedia Commons. Salem, Massachusetts.

Horse and Carriage, Dreamstime.

New York Crystal Palace, Beinecke Rare Book and Manuscript Library, Yale University.

North Church in Salem.

Norwalk Rail Disaster illustration source unknown, public domain.

An exhaustive effort has been made to locate the rights holder for the photograph of the Edwin Bartlett residence (Rockwood Estate) and to clear reprint permission. If the required acknowledgments have been omitted, or any right overlooked, it is unintentional and understanding is requested. The image of Rockwood was found in "Gervase Wheeler, A British Architect in America 1847-1860, Tribert and O'Gorman, Wesleyan University Press, Middletown, Connecticut. 2012.

Salem Harbor by American artist Fitz Hugh Lane.

Tea and Toilet Sets advertised in Sears Roebuck Catalog No. III page 797.

Daguerreotypes of Edward and Lizzie are from personal family collections.

Maps and hats rendered by Elisabeth Johnson based on historic resources.

All other illustrations from Victorian Picture Library except U.S. currency.

Will You Marry Me?

BOOK TWO

The Courtship of Lizzie Andrews

PJ Watters

with Elisabeth Johnson

Acknowledgments

Lizzie's son, Thomas Edward, carefully typed his mother's love letters from Edward Jarvis Tenney exactly as he found them. Thank you, "Grandpa Tommy," for your care in preserving the contents of the fragile letters so we have this story today. Thomas bundled the letters together and tucked them away in his attic, along with daguerreotypes of Lizzie and Edward.

Thank you, Edward, for writing in the raw, real, honest way you did.

Thank you, cousin, Andy Martin, for caring enough to send that "box of stuff" you found in your father's attic to your aunt Elisabeth.

Thank you, Mom, for researching all 200 people Edward mentions in his letters, even though that required more than a decade. Your perseverance in tapping the rich resources in the public domain, and insisting on locating primary sources from genealogy databases, allowed us to piece together the puzzle of Lizzie's and Edward's lives and tell this story. You have compiled an outstanding resource in *Who's Who in Edward Jarvis Tenney's Letters* at pjwattersbooks.com. Thank you.

Thank you, Nan for your patience and guidance as we navigated each step toward publication.

Finally, we are immensely grateful for the ongoing encouragement and feedback from our enthusiastic manuscript readers Barb Willis, Mary McCheyne, Sandy Murphy, Debra Sebanc and Teri Mathis. Thank you.

Last, but certainly not least, we are indebted to our outstanding proofreader Kathy Johnson. Thank you.

Contents

Acknowledgments iv

Prologue ix

I. Shifting Direction

Chapter 1 Senior Year at Harvard 3

Chapter 2 Henry and Emily Oliver 37

Chapter 3 Death's Scourge 55

Chapter 4 The Patient Waiter Is No Loser 63

Chapter 5 Should Not Fear to Die 69

Chapter 6 Give up my Profession 75

II. Secretly Bethrothed

Chapter 7 I Never Knew Joy Before 102

Chapter 8 Love Before Work or Play 112

Chapter 9 Think of You Every Moment 121

Chapter 10 Fear You Are in Danger 125

Chapter 11 Meet Accidentally 133

Chapter 12 Dream Life 139

Chapter 13 Live in Hope 143

III. Death & Deception

Chapter 14 Little Frankie Allen 151

Chapter 15 Breach of Confidence 159

Chapter 16 Say Nothing of It 165

Chapter 17 Rockwood Estate 169

Chapter 18 Call for You at Miss Ward's 179

Chapter 19 Bleak House 185

Chapter 20 The White Hat 195

Chapter 21 Mr. Clinton 203

List of Illustrations

Family Relationship Charts

How Edward J. Tenney & Lizzie Andrews are related — viii
Relationship Chart — 89

Daguerreotypes

Edward Jarvis Tenney 1851 — 1
Lizzie Andrews — 102

Maps

Methuen Village about 1853 — 2
Salem 1851 — 43
Valparaiso, Chile, South America — 94
Massachusetts and Nearby States — 120

Illustrations

B & M Railroad at Hamilton — 8
Beadle's Dime Ball-Room Companion and Guide to Dancing — 15
Hamilton Hall — 19
North Church in Salem — 26
Sears catalog dinner and toilet sets — 27
United States currency — 36
Edward driving his sister's friends home — 68
Joe plays with the children — 72
Norwalk rail disaster — 74
Methuen Congregational Church service — 97
Lizzie waters Aunt Eliza's garden — 99
Celebrating Edward's class-day — 108
Emily Oliver with a basket of daffodils — 119
Salem Harbor — 132
Lizzie embroidering — 138
Lizzie with a love letter — 142

Bad news in a letter	148
Lizzie shares a letter with her sister Laura	158
Railway station ticket office	161
Rockwood Estate on the Hudson River	168
New York Crystal Palace	176
Children in Miss Ward's School	183
Methuen Train Depot	184
Claflin-Richards House in Wenham	190
Men's white hats	194

How *Edward J. Tenney* & *Lizzie Andrews* are related

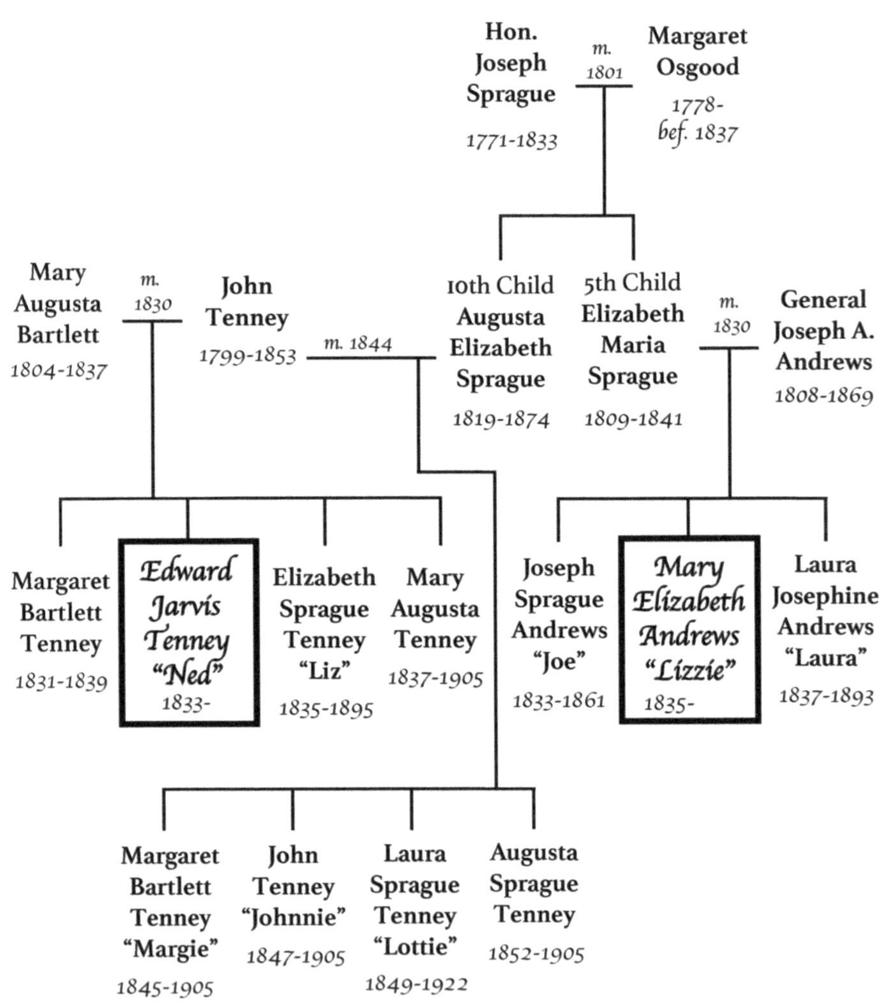

Prologue

"**B**ully for him!" That is what my brother Joe said when I told him Edward was returning to Harvard for his senior year. This past year, Joe spent eleven months at McLean Asylum in Somerville being treated for melancholy; whereas, our cousin Edward was re-admitted to Harvard in Cambridge. Yes, *re-admitted* after being dismissed for refusing to disclose the names of members of his secret society. Edward and two chums were detained by the police during an episode of disorderly conduct and intoxication. He left school, embarrassed and disgraced, and stopped writing me. I feared he was courting someone else. He finally wrote to inform me his father, who is a Massachusetts State Senator, secured his admission to continue his studies at Quaboag Seminary in Warren. Then, Edward departed Harvard a second time when his father became ill.

"Will he stay *this* time?" Joe asked, after hearing of Edward's return. My brother should understand the eldest son must follow his father to support his household. Such responsibility is a new concept for Joe.

At home in Methuen, Edward accompanied Reverend Phillip's daughter Margie horseback riding. She told me she was very fond of Edward. I feared they had become engaged. People were beginning to talk.

As for me, I completed my studies at Miss Ward's School for girls, which is conveniently located right next door to my home in Salem. Now, I commute by train to Hamilton to study to become a teacher. I am an apprentice teacher at Miss Ward's School on Fridays and teach Sunday school. This leaves little time for leisure and dancing at Hamilton Hall.

My father is a shipping merchant, a General and a Justice of the Peace. His sister, Aunt Eliza, has lived with us since my mother died when I was six. Joe was eight and Laura only four. Father never re-married.

Edward was just three when his mother died. His father married my mother's sister Augusta. Edward was ten when she became his mother.

Joe calls us motherless cousins, rich with aunts.

Edward has written me 18 letters since he went away to Harvard two years ago. I saved every one. I am now 17, and I may be falling in love.

I. Shifting Direction

Edward Jarvis Tenney has left his father's bedside in Methuen and returned to Harvard. When he does, his life begins to shift direction.

Edward Jarvis Tenney 1851

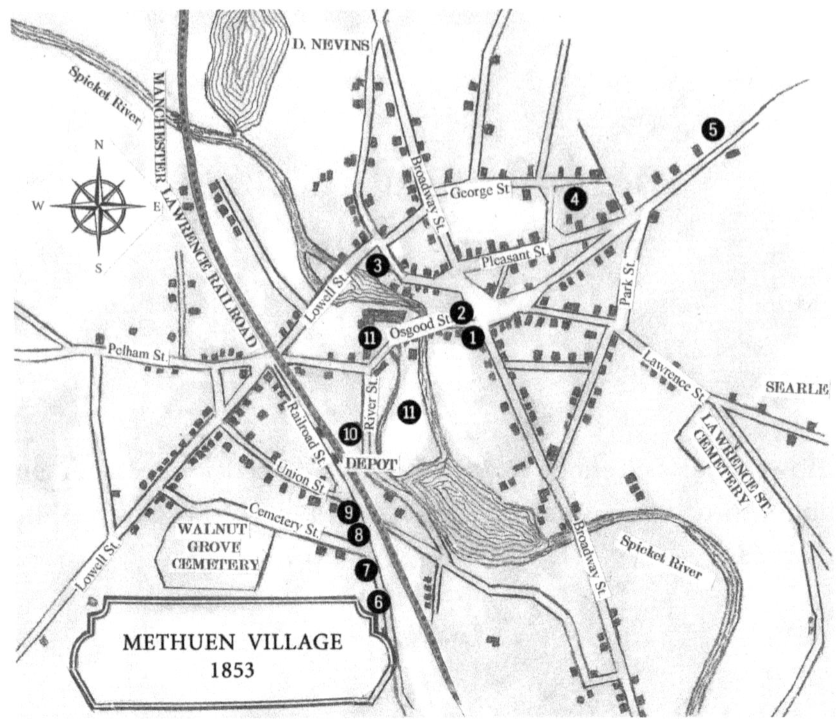

Methuen Village about 1853

❶ Home of Benjamin Osgood

❷ Old Town Hall and Post Office

❸ Methuen Company Store: grocery, hardware, grain (perhaps John F. Tenney grocery store)

❹ Congregational Church

❺ Rev. J.C. Phillips

❻ James Richardson

❼ William Russ, Mayor

❽ David Richardson

❾ John Tenney, Lawyer

❿ John Ferguson Tenney

⓫ Methuen Cotton Mills

CHAPTER 1

Senior Year at Harvard

Miss M. E. Andrews
Care of Gen. Andrews
Salem
Mass.

Cambridge, [Tuesday] Sept. 14th 1852

Dear Cousin -

Oh! College life is charming! Here is one of its oft occurring, pet delights, which always seem to happen so very a'propos. I had my letter but half dated when out goes my lamp and I have to spend half an hour before I can begin again. (I wish my "Goody" was an engineer). But this is nothing. I shall expect a score of classmates to bore me before I am done.

For the first time since I entered college (a long time ago!) I have this year a decent looking room on the first floor, furnished quite prettily and very comfortably. My chum Davies Wilson has a piano and any quantity of music. When you come to Boston this fall, I shall insist upon your seeing the room.

Of course I can't help studying very hard now. To be sure, thus far I have been too busy to study much; for in addition to the usual duties of the first of the term, no sooner had I joined my class than I was requested to write and deliver an oration before a society to which I belong. As this is an honor, I could not refuse; so I worked hard till last Friday night.

You can't possibly guess what my studies for this year are. Besides the regular studies I have chosen, as extra, Italian and Hebrew. The Prof. thinks I am going to be a Unitarian minister. In fact my success in this language is tending to make me change from the law to preaching. Would you? At any rate I am going to be pedagogue this winter, provided I can obtain a school. Wilson, too, will try once more to teach, but he usually trains so much among the young ladies of his school, that he does not teach much.

When you come to Boston, I have any quantity of Concert tickets for you. Germanian, Musical Fund Rehearsal and concert, Serenade Band &c. I am going to the Ser. Band concert tomorrow afternoon with three or four classmates. Can't you possibly be there? August Fries has returned from Europe and will direct the M. Fund. I am sorry for it, because we shall lose his fine music at rehearsals and concerts for the sake of directing which some one else might do as well as he. Mlle Lehman is to come soon and will sing all winter for the Quintette club. Madame Thillon will not be in Boston before October, if then even. Sontag and Alboni will be here after the music hall is completed. You must be prepared to stay a long while in Boston when you come and come you will, 'of course.'

15th   I intended to have written you earlier, but have been so very busy, and I knew that you were in no hurry, that I have postponed it from day to day without thinking how fast fled time. On that Tuesday I reached the cars just in time and arrived at home a few moments before father. The next day I decided to go back to college and I left home the Wednesday following, without another farewell ride with Margie Phillips or even seeing her before my departure. That was not my fault however, for she was at Lowell Island.

Liz writes me that Margie & herself have rode alone since I left. Have you forgotten to make some arrangement about attending riding school? I wish that you could come to Boston once a week for that purpose. Only think! If you do, you can ride from Boston to Salem with Theo. A.!!! You can't resist that temptation I know.

One poor freshman from Salem was treated dreadfully by the Sophomores last night. He is Devereux, so Oliver says. It was raining and about midnight the Sophs carried him from his room and tied him so firmly to a tree in the yard that he remained out doors a long time before he could extricate himself. This might have killed him, and it far exceeds any college barbarity I ever heard of. I have not heard of Geo. Holyoke's being troubled at all yet.

I wrote to Joe some time ago, but I fear he will not like the tone of my letter. I wrote what your father asked me to and I told J. that he must do something soon if he would keep away from Somerville.

Don't think I am falling off in the length of my letters; for this is only once.

Do write as soon as you can and a very long letter. Say when you will be in Boston.

Good bye, Cura cuzina -

Ever yours
Edward

Remember! You must come to Boston before Thanksgiving. I am expecting Carrie Wilson at my room with her brother every moment, and he says she will exercise his piano for the next two hours. Excuse my writing but I have scratched this last page in great haste, for fear of Miss W's coming.

Friday, 17 September 1852

As I head out the door to catch an early-morning train, Father advises me, "Lizzie, my dear girl, pay attention to your studies."

"Of course, Father. Good bye."

His command echoes in my ears as I scurry down Chestnut Street to the train station. Pay attention to my studies? That would be easier if Father had not just handed me Edward's letter this morning. He knows I am more than fond of my cousin and cherish his letters. He knows…I wonder just how much he *does* know about me and my kissing cousin Edward.

Father was so nonchalant when he delivered the letter this morning. "Lizzie, here is a letter to you from your cousin Edward. Perhaps you would like to read it on the train," he said. "Or, shall I put it in your room, so you can read it when you return?" What was he thinking? How could he torment me so?

"Thank you, Father. I would much prefer to read it on the train," I responded just as nonchalantly. I had to muster every ounce of free will I could to silence my questions: Could Father have picked up the mail on Thursday afternoon and forgotten to give me my letter? Forgotten? Father? Never! Not the General. He simply never forgets. I have learned only to question Father when he invites my inquiries.

I loosen the ties on my satchel and tuck Edward's letter safely inside, observing that Edward did indeed pre-pay the three-cent postage, which is something Father would notice.

Edward is honest and noble. Perhaps his calling is indeed to become a Unitarian minister. Father says Harvard's first benefactor was a Unitarian clergyman. He told me the college was founded to train clergy to educate the Puritans, using the benefactor's donated library. Of course, the library has expanded much in the past 200 years ago.

Looking up, I notice the leaves on the trees have not yet changed color. The air is brisk. The colors will change soon. Today, the canopy of leaves above the street shades the sun and freckles the pavers on Chestnut Street. My feet navigate the uneven surface and I pick up my pace to ensure I reach my train on time.

My short walk takes me past two of my favorite buildings—Hamilton Hall, where I dance, and the post office, where I mail and receive letters. As I approach the Salem station, I hear, "All aboard for Wenham, Hamilton and Ipswich." I hurry to a car near the back of the train and climb aboard, far from the risk of ash, which can spew from the coal engine and deposit soot or burn holes in a silk dress. As the car jerks forward, I pull Edward's letter from my bag and quietly unfold the pages to savor his message.

All too soon, the train arrives at the Hamilton Depot and I dash to school, eager to discuss the literary works of authors Washington Irving or Edgar Allan Poe. Father would be proud! This summer we were to read a book by one of these authors, and as I find Poe rather frightful and macabre, I opted for Irving's *Rip Van Winkle*. This story of immense imagination tempts the reader to ponder how one could completely escape a difficult time in history, or in one's life, through oversleeping. I think my brother Joe may have done just that this past year! Lo, that I could sleep away the time until I can become Edward's wife and establish a home with a family of my own. Father's warning echoes through my head, "Pay attention to your studies." Yes, Father, I respond to myself, appeasing his voice in my head. Adding a message to Father, for good measure, I am certain we will also discuss the headless horseman in *The Legend of Sleepy Hollow*. I read that book over the summer, as well.

B & M Railroad at Hamilton

Sunday, 19 September 1852

In my room, on this most pleasant fall afternoon, I change from my church dress to a simple day dress, and settle at my writing desk. Glancing out the window, I see the weather is nearly nice enough to sit in the garden. However, I am eager to respond to Edward's letter, so opt to forsake the purple asters, which I notice still look very lovely in Aunt Eliza's flower bed. Words pour onto the paper as if I were spending the afternoon conversing with my dear cousin.

We are returning to some semblance of normalcy, I tell him, with you at Cambridge, I at Hamilton and Laura at Miss Ward's finishing school.

Joe is fond of asking Laura, "When will you be *finished*, Laura?" He can be very funny at times. Laura takes him literally. "Not just yet, Joe," she responds in all sincerity. My sister is a sweet girl. I admit I missed my brother's clever quips when he was gone. Now that he is home from Somerville I pray he will make something of himself. In fact, his return nearly demands he do so, though he has not yet engaged in any worthwhile vocation. I thank God Joe is not at college! Oh, my gracious, what an ordeal we might have on our hands if that were the case! Joe would ne'er survive the antics at Harvard. Surely, he'd be the first one selected to be doused with a bucket of water or tied to a tree!

Monday, 20 September 1852

I met my friend Emily Oliver at the train station this morning. I was waiting to depart for Hamilton. She was just in from Lawrence. We spoke of the rambunctious ordeal pertaining to Mr. Devereux, without speaking his name aloud, of course.

"Your brother told Edward of a most-shocking incident on campus," I informed Emily. Her brother, Henry, is studying at Harvard to become a doctor. I described all I had heard.

"His only crime was having been born the son of a prominent man," she exclaimed.

"Well, I think the scholars' behavior is barbaric and even shameful!"

"When will someone put an end to such rowdy behavior?" she asks.

"I certainly hope the authorities at Harvard will." I thought of Edward's dismissal and added, in a whisper, "They have been known to take more drastic action for a lesser crime."

"Absurd!" she declares, knowing the incident to which I refer.

"Actually, Edward is fortunate. Contrary to this situation, my dear cousin was celebrated by his Harvard chums, hoisted up like a dignitary and carried by the crowd the morning he left campus. Did you know a fine barouche-and-four appeared at the college gate to parade him and the other two expelled scholars around the grounds?"

"Edward never told me about that," she replied. "Where did the barouche end up?"

"They were set down with much ceremony at the Revere House in Boston."

"I can imagine him parked in front." She smiled. "Now, when I pass the Revere House, I will likely think of Edward, rather than Paul Revere!"

"I hope he does not mind me sharing such stories with you."

"Do not worry, Lizzie, I will tease him only a bit when I see him."

"Emily! You dare not!" I protested.

"Alright, I will tease him *a lot*!" she said, as a train screeched into the station. "There is my train to Boston, Lizzie." She bid me good-bye and left me with a smile that assured me I could trust her. "Do not worry!"

⸻ ⟨ೞ⟩ ⸻

Thursday, 23 September 1852

Meeting an acquaintance like Emily at the train makes my frequent travels so much more enjoyable. However, on the train or at the station, I am always prepared with a good book. This week, I found *Uncle Tom's Cabin* to be a fitting companion.

Upon my return from Hamilton at week's end, I descend from the train platform at the Washington Street Station, and walk along Chestnut Street. Enjoying another beautiful day, I make a detour at Crombie Street for an uninvited appearance at Grandmother's house, just in time for tea.

As I approach the house, I see an unfamiliar carriage parked in front. It is beautifully adorned. I greet the driver, and the horse to ensure I do not startle him, lingering to marvel at the scene painted upon the carriage door. Two ladies and their escorts walk down a garden path; a lush wooded area looms behind them as they head toward a bright and prettily displayed floral garden. I select one gentleman to be Edward, and picture myself on his arm. My daydream is interrupted as a voice sounds from the house. Grandmother sings out through the open window, "Lizzie, is that you, my dear?"

"Yes, it is I." I turn and hurry up the short walk hoping Grandmother has not seen me dilly-dallying. The moment I close the front door, she calls out again, gently demanding, "Come, dear, join me for tea and scones." I greet her in the parlor. The smell of fresh scones wafts through the air. Oh, how I love tea time at Grandmother's house.

"Greetings, Grandmother." Grandmother sits in an arm chair by the tea cart. I give her a peck on each cheek, and turn to greet Aunt Dolly, who sits a few feet away at the dining room table. Next to her is a woman in a fashionable hat who I suspect is one of her millinery customers and the owner of the beautiful carriage.

"Hello, Lizzie," Aunt Dolly says. Speaking to the lady in the hat, she continues, "This is my niece Mary Elizabeth, just home from school in Hamilton." To me, she says, "Lizzie, meet Mrs. Porter. She came from Boston for a brand-new hat, having seen the one I made for her sister in Salem." Mrs. Porter appears pleased with her purchase.

"Nice to meet you, Mrs. Porter."

"Nice to meet you, too, Lizzie. I trust your travels were fine on such a beautiful day."

"Yes, indeed. Thank you, Mrs. Porter."

Aunt Dolly primps a piece of netting from the back of the new hat's wide brim, so it drapes down just enough to reach the top of Mrs. Porter's jacket collar.

"That is a lovely hat, Mrs. Porter."

"Thank you, Lizzie," a beaming Mrs. Porter replies, causing Aunt Dolly to smile. Aunt Dolly's smile includes one or two hat pins, which she bites tightly between her teeth. She seems pleased to be engaging a new customer, and smiling, for she has lost a few patrons lately who have fallen onto hard times.

"Have I not seen your hat style in *Godey's Lady's Book*?" I ask.

"Certainly not, Lizzie," Dolly says, no longer smiling. "The design is an original for Mrs. Porter. You will not see the likes of it anywhere else."

"The style looks particularly lovely on you, Mrs. Porter," I confirm, and manage to get a bit of a smile back on Aunt Dolly's face.

"Come sit by me, dear. Have some tea and a scone." Grandmother pats the cushion next to her on the davenport. I sit, facing my plate. The butter melts immediately on the hot scone, and I take a bite.

"Grandmother, your scones are the best! They are a perfect texture and density. May I have your recipe for Bridget?"

"You may have it for yourself," she replies. I know she likes our Irish servant Bridget, but Grandmother insists that I not be completely dependent on cooks and housekeepers to assure my 'independent self-sufficiency.' She immediately begins reciting the recipe. I reach to pull a sheet of paper from my bag to write upon and look around for an inkwell. She remarks, "Lizzie, no need to write anything down. You can recall this easily, for the recipe is simple. You must train your mind to remember." After reciting the ingredients, she leans toward me and says, "The secret is using very cold butter and baking in an extremely hot oven."

That completed, I finish my scone and engage her with a reading from my school papers. Before I depart, I share the news from Hamilton—of which there is not much my grandmother would care to know. I promise to return on Sunday after church for a nice long visit.

<hr>

Sunday, 26 September 1852

I spend the whole of my free afternoon at Grandmother's reading poetry to her by Thoreau and Longfellow. I am not sure she is ready for fiction as progressive as *Uncle Tom's Cabin*. She keeps her hands busy crocheting, explaining to me, "Idle hands are the devil's workshop, and besides," she confesses, "my hands stiffen up if I do not keep them moving."

I read, "I hear the sweet evening sounds; From your undecaying grounds; Cheat me no more with time; Take me to your clime." I conclude Thoreau's poem, "All Things Are Current Found" and ask, "Are you tiring of having me read aloud?"

"Oh no, dear, you read more rapidly than my old eyes can see; and I enjoy the presence of your company just as well as the poetry."

"Shall I read Longfellow now? Autumn, Voices of the Night," I begin, "With what a glory comes and goes the year!"

Upon my return home, I poke my head into Father's library to greet him, and move quietly to my room to ready for supper. Joe, in sharp contrast, arrives home just after me, parades by with full sound effects and demands immediate attention to some issue that holds no urgency.

When I return downstairs to join my family in the parlor, Laura is scrutinizing Joe as he pulls the linings from his trouser pockets and leaves them out to flop at his sides like rabbit ears.

"Laura, did someone send all my handkerchiefs to the laundress? I cannot find a one." He seems truly distressed.

"The laundress was here yesterday. Did you set them out to be laundered?" She answers, not expecting a response, and continues to turn the pages in the latest *Godey's Lady's Book*. Joe does not leave and manages to make the mystery of the disappearing handkerchiefs an issue for the entire family. Hearing the disturbance, Father appears and says, "Do you have a sufficient supply, Joe? If you are to carry a clean one daily, you may need more."

"I believe I have a good number; however, many of them appear to have sprouted legs and gone into hiding." He wipes his nose on his sleeve and wanders toward the kitchen.

Joe seems to be missing more than his handkerchief. What occupation could he pursue when he cannot find his own handkerchief? Perhaps, since he is expected to set his sights much farther and wider than a young lady's, he fails to see what is right before him.

***

Saturday, 2 October 1852

After supper, Father and Joe join Aunt Eliza, Laura and me in the parlor amid much discussion about Laura and my plans to go dancing at Hamilton Hall. When Aunt Dolly arrives to visit for the evening, Laura and I excuse ourselves to dress for the dance. I follow Laura up the stairs, overhearing the conversations fading behind us.

"Lizzie is becoming so much like her mother," Aunt Eliza says.

"She is quite a lady," Father agrees.

Aunt Dolly joins in, "Do you realize what fine skills she has acquired in sewing and knitting?"

Aunt Eliza's voice fades as she says, "She certainly has taken a liking to her dancing lessons."

I feel a flush rise to my face, as if I were still in the room, which, if I were, would have embarrassed me to no end. To me, dancing is at least as necessary as sewing, cooking and literature for a lady. Some days, reading my dance card is more interesting than my favorite book. Thank goodness I have had no shortage of escorts for this activity, and the opportunities in Hamilton are nearly as plentiful as those in Salem. This will be Laura's first dance, however, so I need to help her prepare not only her attire, but also ensure she feels completely comfortable with the etiquette of the dance.

As we retreat into the bedroom, I close the door and ask, "Laura, do you feel confident with the steps you have learned?"

"I have many steps yet to learn, yet feel I will be able to follow. My lack of knowledge about steps causes me to feel less nervous than forgetting what to say, or speaking when I should not."

"Sit here on the bed, Laura and practice with me. I will be the gentleman."

I approach her, stopping about three feet away, bow forward across my folded left arm, present my right hand slightly and ask, "Will you do me the honor of a dance with me?" Laura does not reply immediately, so I add, "for this or the next dance?" Still bent forward, hearing no response, I continue, "May I have the kind pleasure of signing your dance card?"

"Oh, Lizzie, how do I accept? Do I just say 'yes'?" Laura crumbles, and looks to be near tears. "I've gone and ruined my first dance already!"

"That is why we are practicing, Laura. First, you must give him the courtesy of a timely response," I tried not to sound like I was chastising her. "Let's trade places and you ask me." She stood, and I sat on the edge of the bed. Now, ask me if I will do you the honor to dance with you."

"Will you do me the honor to dance with me?" she bows forward and closes her eyes. I whisper to her, "A gentleman will continue to look at you when he bows so he can see your response." She looks up, and I respond, "It would be my pleasure." I pretend to pick up my dance card

*Beadle's Dime Ball-Room Companion and
Guide to Dancing*

and hand it to her, "However, I am promised for the next dance," I say. "I would be delighted if you would sign my dance card, and call on me again."

Laura looks so disappointed I wish I had simply said, "Yes." I assure her it is most appropriate to offer such a response. She pretends to pick up my card and lifts the imaginary pencil that would typically hang from the card on a ribbon and initials my card.

"Let's switch places again," I insist and stand to guide her to the edge of the bed.

"Will you favor me with your hand for the next dance?" I ask.

"Yes," she replies, reaching out her hand and beginning to rise to her feet. "May I just say that, Lizzie? Or should I say, 'It would be my pleasure.'"

"A simple 'yes' is a lovely response, Laura."

"What if a gentleman I do not know asks me to dance?"

"There will be many you do not know, as this is your first dance, but a gentleman will likely ask for an introduction from one of his friends, or the floor manager, before he asks you to dance. You will have opportunities to talk before someone asks you to dance, but do not worry, he should not become too familiar! After you dance, he should never leave you on the dance floor. He will offer his arm to escort you back to your seat or if your seat has been subsequently occupied, he will find you another seat. He should not occupy a seat next to you, however."

"He shouldn't?"

"Now, if he asks you again right away, you must offer your card instead, so as not to appear too eager to dance with only one partner. You may dance with someone three or four times at most throughout the evening."

"Even if he is my escort?"

"If he is your escort, he will know not to occupy all your time. He is your escort *to* the dance hall, not your escort for every dance." We continue to talk as we dress. I lace Laura's corset for her, but she insists on speaking and will not hold her breath long enough for me to snug all the laces.

"Lizzie, have you received a letter from our cousins Liz or Edward lately? I have not heard from Mary for some time. I wonder how their father fares."

"I have not heard a word for more than two weeks," I responded. "Now, hold still."

"Do you think Uncle John will die?" she asks, much to my surprise. Why is she thinking of this as we prepare for a pleasant evening out? Laura was only four when our mother died, and she says she does not remember her much at all. I think one never fully recovers from the loss of a family member. Laura is a very compassionate sort and is wondering about her cousin Mary.

"Uncle John will die someday, of course. We all will, but I think he is feeling better," I reply, though I do not know how well he really is.

Laura's concern was not abated. "What will Aunt Augusta do if he dies while the children are so young?" Edward, Liz and Mary's half siblings are all under the age of eight.

We pulled Laura's dress over her head, and I proceeded to fasten the long row of buttons that descend from the nape of her neck to her waist.

"At least Aunt Augusta has Edward to care for her." I mean to sound reassuring, but am not even convincing myself.

"Let me tie up your hair now, Laura." She hands me her hairbrush, and I begin stroking her long blond hair to gather every strand into a tail. I pull it up and twist it into a tight knot. She hands me a ribbon to secure it in place and continues her chatter.

"Oh, I pray no harm befalls our father, for we could not depend on Joe to care for us! We would be orphans, Lizzie! Would we have to find a family who needs a nanny to make ourselves useful?"

Her questions cannot be easily answered. I recall Joe saying he cannot post a letter to Edward because he does not have a half-dime to his name, and he certainly is not going to seek assistance from Father who would thereby subject him to a grand inquisition as to where he had expended his allowance. Despite my own concerns, I try my best to reassure Laura, "We would move in with Grandmother. Certainly, Uncle Daniel could take care of us."

"And Aunt Eliza, Aunt Dolly, Grandmother and Joe? All of us?" she says, showing she had thought this through.

"Laura, you worry too much! Joe will learn to support himself soon. We will surely both marry before Father passes away. He is healthy and hardy, like Grandmother. She shows no signs of succumbing to anything! Now lace my corset, Laura. We must not dally any longer."

"It is not easy for a woman with no man to take care of her, is it, Lizzie?" She lifts my dress over my head. I cannot answer until the full skirt is past my face and has fallen into place over my crinoline and petticoats. We each wear two underskirts, for this will be our costume for a special occasion. We need to practice dancing in so many layers.

"Let me look at you, Laura. You are so very lovely."

She beams, and responds, "You look like a princess, Lizzie."

Once readied, we hurry to greet our escorts, George and his younger brother Charles, our neighbor Rose Lee's brothers. As we descend the stairs, we can hear they are being adequately interrogated in the foyer by Father and Joe. For a second, I imagine I am actually meeting Edward for the dance or a Serenade Band concert. Then I remember he does not dance much. Therefore, I will dance with George today and listen to the concert with Edward later; I conclude in my fantasy.

No one comments on the dresses Laura and I wore, but I watch for a reaction. I do not avert my eyes readily any more, believing a lady misses too much with youthful modesty. Charles' mouth falls slightly open as he helps Laura with her wrap. She does not notice. He does not miss her radiance. Her blond hair looks so sleek. She puts on her bonnet and ties the lace in a loose bow under her chin, discreetly avoiding his eye contact. Her face looks tiny as she peers out from her bonnet brim.

We walk together toward Hamilton Hall. The evening is crisp and clear, perfect for an evening out. George initiates a conversation to fill the short time before we will be silenced by the music emanating from the hall. Laura and Charles trail slightly behind us.

"Lizzie, do you teach Sunday school tomorrow?" George asks.

"Yes, I do. I quite enjoy working with the little children."

"I hope you will not be too tired from dancing."

Did he think me so frail I could not dance an entire evening? "I am certain I will not. Rather than succumb to tiredness, I fully expect to have more vitality from all the activity."

"Well, I think it grand that your father allows you and Laura to come out tonight."

"Though Father expects much from us, he is not concerned in any manner about us partaking in activities we enjoy. I suppose we are fortunate in this. Just the other day I overheard a conversation on the train of a poor girl whose father prohibits her from not only dancing but also the enjoyment of listening to music."

Hamilton Hall

"Is that so?" George seems to be sincerely interested, so I continue.

"Her entire day was filled with stillness and silence—her only attention being to read her Bible. She reads it morning, noon and night. By the end of each year, she had re-read the entire Good Book cover to cover. She did this year after year! Is it not absurd that some find listening to music and dancing immoral, in this day and age?"

George responds, "I read the Bible, over and again. Nowhere have I found those activities to be a sin. Of course, I do not read it in such a regimented manner. Perhaps, I have missed something."

As George speaks, I realize what I have missed. Edward! I love that country cousin of mine. I recall Edward telling me to 'give his love to all.' He warns me not to give *away* all his love, however. Rather, he insists I keep as much of it for myself as I can manage.

George is a fine escort, and I enjoy him as a dance partner, but he is not Edward.

That is the great sin in *my* life—not that I dance, but that I cannot find occasion to christen the dance hall in Edward's arms. How ludicrous that George takes me to dance and Edward accompanies Margie for horseback rides when we would both enjoy so much spending those times together. I hope he wishes she were me on those outings, as I dream it was he who would promenade me across the floor boards at Hamilton Hall or Papanti's.

Tuesday, 5 October 1852

At Father's request, I did not return to Hamilton yesterday. I delayed my departure to celebrate the 47th anniversary of the formation of the Salem Light Infantry. We spent the afternoon at the encampment with Aunt Eliza, Laura and Joe, where we met Emily Oliver. Our families sat together in the stands while Father and Emily's father, General Henry Kemble Oliver, engaged in reviewing the troops.

Many other officers were present conducting drills. The soldiers paraded in formation while the drill sergeants inspected their appearance, walking up and down the lines seemingly very aware that all eyes in the stands were on them. Not a single soldier smiled, and Laura was very concerned that they were not enjoying the ceremonies.

"They are not supposed to smile, Laura," I explained. "They will smile later—after their officers tell them how well they marched."

That evening the Salem Light Infantry and the Providence Light Infantry marched to Hamilton Hall amid a blaze of fireworks and colored torchlights, followed by a vast throng of spectators. As we arrived, the soldiers greeted their families and filled the tables in the hall to enjoy a banquet of meats, fresh fruits and plenty to drink. There were so many soldiers! Emily and I admired them all, but not nearly as much as the soldiers seemed to admire my sister Laura. She appeared to be enamored by all of them. As I had predicted, there was no shortage of smiles. I did not see Charlie Pierson this year, as I often do. However, among the distinguished guests was Lieutenant Leverett Saltonstall of the New England Guards.

Seeing Leverett, I recalled the horrific incident during a party at my home when my brother insulted Leverett, accusing him of expressing inappropriate affections toward my friend Rose Lee. Leverett's father is a former Salem Mayor and, although his son is nearly a decade older than Rose, he is certainly well-mannered, which made my brother's behavior appear all the more barbaric. I was not surprised to see Rose attending the ceremonies and I sought her out to exchange pleasantries.

⎯⎯⎯⎯⎯❧⎯⎯⎯⎯⎯

Saturday, 16 October 1852

For three weeks, each Sabbath has been filled from dawn to dusk with activities. I teach Sunday school in the morning and spend afternoons with family, reading, writing or embroidering. Monday through Thursday, I catch the early train to Hamilton and return to Salem after dusk in the evening. On Friday, I teach at Miss Ward's School, which leaves only Saturday to prepare for the next week's lessons. All this allows no luxury of time to visit Edward or attend a concert in Boston. I have no time to take a horseback lesson, though I would enjoy nothing more. Well, to be certain, there is something I would enjoy more. Neither activity brings me as much pleasure as dancing. I do wish my dear cousin Edward would learn to dance.

Mary Thompson tells me she saw Edward leave our house last Wednesday evening. Sadly, I missed him for I had not yet returned from Hamilton that evening. To his good fortune, our neighbor recognized him and did not mistake him for someone lurking about our house after dark when no one was home. When Laura and I are away, Aunt Eliza goes to the Andrews family home to be in the company of her mother and sister Dolly. She likes to cook and bake, so usually prepares both dinner and supper for Grandmother, Dolly and Daniel.

I understand Edward's surprise to find our home closed up and empty last Wednesday, as this is quite rare, even during the winters when I board in Hamilton to avoid the perils of winter train travel. Father spends so much time at his office in Boston, he is often away from home. Still, usually someone is at home. We have three servants— Bridget and Margo, who cook and clean, and Father's new valet Edward Clark, whose duties include tending to the horse and carriage. Joe is not one to help much. Father tries to coach him in hopes he might one day function as the head of a household. I hardly think my brother Joe

21

could be a 'man of the house.' Though he is older than I am, he still behaves like a boy.

Last Saturday, Father spoke with Joe and me about how our house, built just seven years ago in 1845, might be in need of updating to accommodate modern conveniences. Perhaps all his time in Boston has him thinking about this! Only a few new houses are being built in Salem now during this depression. Those that have been newly erected are filled with the same amenities we have seen in the fine hotels in New York, such as pipes along the walls that carry gas to fuel the lights. There is no need to fill the lamps with oil! Some new houses have a tank for boiling water that flows through pipes into each room of the house to provide heat. Imagine that, heat without a fire in the room! There are also pipes for water one can drink—not just at the kitchen-sink pump. Water can even be pumped to rooms upstairs!

Father might fit our home with a necessary room right indoors. Our servants would no longer need to empty chamber pots. Not only would a necessary room replace chamber pots, but there would be no need for an outhouse. I am grateful not to leave the house entirely at night, especially in the winter. I cannot think how this would work, but I have seen it done!

On my next trip to Boston, I must observe more carefully the advances that have been made in hotel accommodations. I have made arrangements to go with Father so often and then cancelled my plans, even after telling Edward of them. I truly enjoy my schooling and teaching at Miss Ward's and Sunday school, so am loathe to give up anything! Even Father's offers to join him, and Edward's encouragement to visit, have not pulled me away from my routine for a quick trip to Boston. Perhaps if Kate could meet me there, the thought of her meeting my cousin would provide the impetus I need. Kate would ask the boldest questions of Edward's feelings and intentions and he would undoubtedly reveal his affection for me, or dread, perhaps he would admit any reluctance toward betrothal.

⋯⟋⟍⋯

Saturday, 30 October 1852

Father joined me in the parlor this morning where I was planning tomorrow's Sunday school lesson for the children at North Church. My thoughts drifted to planning a trip to Boston. Father snapped the newspaper as he folded it and startled me out of my daydream.

"Lizzie, did you know Secretary Webster was a candidate for President of the United States when he fell from his horse and died last Sunday?"

"Oh, no. What a tragedy!" I thought of all the horseback riding Edward does and his encouragement for me to join him. I added, "I guess such a fate could befall anyone!"

"Certainly prominence is no protection from death," Father replied, and in his pragmatic way changed the focus to the Secretary's life, rather than his death. "Due to the deaths of both Presidents Harrison and Taylor, if Webster had taken the opportunity to serve either man as his vice president, he would have succeeded him to become president. Webster may have been too proud to start out as vice president."

"Too proud? Did you know him, Father?"

"I did not know him personally. He was a Dartmouth alumnus, as was Delevan Mussey's father and Henry Kemble Oliver," he said, naming people I would know, probably to keep my attention. I wondered how Father knew so much about their educational backgrounds. His memory was like an encyclopedia. He continued to talk, "Webster was a good friend to shipping interests and to mill owners, but he lost many supporters when he spoke in favor of the Fugitive Slave Act. His politics drew admirers and critics, but no one doubted his impact as a leader. He was a great compromiser and many who oppose slavery did not welcome his argument that tolerating slavery in the southern states is the only way to save our union."

I tried to recall what I had read about the abolition of slavery. My knowledge was limited, so I asked, "Father, is it not true that citizens of all states are required to report the comings and goings of free black men, even if they are not runaway slaves?"

"That is correct," Father reinforced me.

"Father, what would happen if a free black man could not verify he was free? Would he be returned to the south?"

"He would. What do you think about that, Lizzie?"

"Well, I guess I feel this would pose a great injustice on free blacks."

"You guess you feel?"

"No, I do feel it is an injustice," I responded, realizing he did not ask about my feelings, but was inquiring as to my thoughts. I continued, "I am quite certain that is what I think, for how could any Christian soul agree to tear any man from his family?" Truth be told, I was feeling upset imagining such a situation.

"Father, how can one person own another person? As a Christian country, how can we sit idly by and turn a blind eye to slavery? Does not the Declaration say human beings possess a right to liberty?" I wondered how I might form this to be an appropriate lesson for Sunday school.

"Yes, life, liberty and the pursuit of happiness are natural rights," Father said. "We also have the right of conscience, and with that right, comes our responsibility. Just as we had to fight to gain our freedom from British rule, a fight over the injustice of slavery may be inevitable. Perhaps Webster's death will quell any outward criticisms of the man."

"Criticism?" I asked.

"I think Webster was seeking a diplomatic solution to slavery that did not involve warfare. Even when we hold common Christian values, we can differ greatly in terms of the strategies we agree to take to accomplish a common goal."

Christian conscience and responsibility, compassion for the most disadvantaged—that would be the basis of my lesson for tomorrow. Father gazed out the window just as Joe walked into the house, and I knew our conversation had concluded. Father does not ask Joe his opinion. Joe walked past the Parlor and into the kitchen without a word. Father rose from his chair and followed Joe. I overheard him greet Joe in a most formal manner that seemed to be Father's attempt to demonstrate common social respect, which is something my brother cannot seem to remember to initiate.

I let out a sigh of relief to overhear Joe and Father engaged in civil discourse; and refocused my attention on finishing my lesson plan. That completed, I pulled out a letter from Kate Pollard. Kate had written me that she hopes to meet in Boston once more with her friend, Ruth Foster, who is engaged to be married on the 20th of November. Ruth is making final preparations and purchasing items for her trousseau and Kate invited me to join them. She says we will have a grand time helping Ruth select the most fashionable styles of kitchen and dining linens. I imagine by the time I arrive, there will not be much left to purchase or prepare.

I began to write her, apologizing for my change of plans two weeks ago and recommitting to meet with her in Boston within a fortnight. If I affirm my intention often enough, I may actually make the trip. I concluded my letter with 'Hopefully, I shall not be deterred by inclement weather, which season is rapidly approaching.'

Both Edward and Kate have been so encouraging of my travels to Boston. I do look forward to introducing Edward to Kate, and Kate to my dear cousin—in the most discreet manner, of course. It affords me the greatest pleasure to speak freely about Edward with any friend who has made his acquaintance. Emily Oliver is a perfect example. It was Edward's strong encouragement to converse with her that led to Emily becoming one of my dearest friends.

North Church in Salem

Sunday, 31 October 1852

After the final child is claimed from the Sunday school classroom by his parents, I am free to enter the church reception hall where I find Emily sitting at the far end of a long table. She has flung her crocheted bag carelessly across the chair next to her. Upon seeing me, she sweeps the bag from the chair and motions me to occupy the seat.

Her voice is low when she greets me. "Hello, Lizzie. How are you?"

"I am quite well, thank you. How are you?" I respond in a similar tone, feeling somewhat silly doing so.

"I am not a bit well."

"Oh?" I try not to be too obtrusive as I scan Emily's face, searching for signs of illness. She looks well. She has a perfectly lovely profile. Her skin is not at all flushed—just a touch of pink in her cheeks, the same rosy color that appears on her lips, which she presses into a thin line, as if she is trying to control a trembling lip. Perhaps she is plagued by her monthly visitor. If so, I hope she has brought a fresh rag and needs no assistance from me in that regard. I glance around to see if the necessary room is occupied should she have to excuse herself.

I invite her to say more. She turns her dark eyes away and appears to be examining her teacup. I glance discretely to confirm her cup and saucer appear to be in satisfactory condition. Of course, I cannot help but notice the China pattern is more traditional than the newer patterns I have seen imported from Limoges, France. I wonder if the church receives donations of older China when parishioners pass away.

Emily's expression is shaded by a light-brown bonnet the same color as her hair, which is pulled smoothly from her face. She turns and looks at me again and pops her fan to cover a smile she can no longer bite back. I see her eyes turn up at the corners and know only then that her comment was in jest.

"Emily, you scoundrel. You are merciless!" I am more relieved than angered. She continues, "I am not well, Lizzie. I have a problem… with

Sears catalog dinner and toilet sets

my insides." Then she quickly adds, "They are completely filled with butterflies!"

What a sight we must be, giggling and carrying on like noisy schoolgirls. We try to muffle our laughter behind our fans. Other ladies are gathering in the room for afternoon tea. Now Emily feigns a sincere tone to explain, "I did not intend to concern you, Lizzie, but I have much to tell you. I am so glad you came to tea today."

"Yes, I have missed tea a few times recently after being detained by a swarm of little ones in Sunday school. Some days, their parents remain long after church service has concluded. So tell me about your butterflies!" I insist.

"First I must tell you that my sister Sarah is engaged to be married!"

"To whom?"

"Joseph Battles." My expression must have revealed the name was unfamiliar to me, so she explains, "He works for my father as the paymaster at the Atlantic Mills."

"That is splendid. Please give him my best regards," I urge her to continue. "Surely that is not the cause of your butterflies."

"True," she says and takes a deep breath. "Father has arranged a rendezvous for me with a gentleman in Salem." She sits smugly, with not another word. She is going to make me ask who!

"Oh, Emily, do not let me intrude on your personal business!" I mock her.

"Of course, I will tell you more, but you must promise not to tell another soul."

"It is done." I cross my heart with my pointer finger on my right hand.

"I am going to meet a 'Mr. Briggs' who has asked my father for permission to see me. Mr. Briggs told Father he saw me and cannot remove from his mind the vision of my loveliness!" She laughs as if hearing his comment for the first time.

"But you are all of that! Was it recently he saw you?"

"Most likely, for I have lived in Lawrence only four years, since my father became superintendent of the Mills."

"Only four years ago?" I asked in surprise.

"Yes. 1848. I was only 11 years old. We moved in the summer. I remember the empty shell of a building that Father said would become a mill. That summer, he did all the work of fitting, setting up and starting the machinery—after selecting the mill overseers, of course. Then, he built a second mill the next year and a third mill a year later!" Now he is planting trees all over the public square in Lawrence."

"Trees? Emily! Is it a forest in the town square?"

"But that is not all, Lizzie. He also established a free library in the mill. He told the overseers that if they organized themselves into a library association, he would commence the library with a donation of one hundred volumes and a loan of $50 for new purchases. This was done and the library has already increased far beyond that with nearly 1,000 volumes."

I could feel Emily's pride in her father. I have felt that same in mine. Emily proceeded to tell me her father also established hot and cold baths in a building at the rear of the mill for the workers to use.

"He seems to be such a kind man, Emily."

"Oh, Lizzie, I have not told you the half of it. My father seems to know what it might be like to be in need. Though I do not know how he could, for we have never wanted for much." She leaned toward me as if to tell me about a scandal of sorts, and she said, "A girl at the factory appropriated a piece of cloth from her loom for her own personal use!"

"Shocking!"

"Yes! She pinned the cloth around her waist, under her clothing. Just as she was leaving the mill-yard at evening, it loosened and dropped upon the ground. Everyone was heading out at the same time. There was no hiding what happened. Father and the overseers were standing at the mill steps, as they usually do, to see the crowd depart. An overseer picked up the cloth and brought the girl to Father."

"Oh no! She must have been mortified!"

"Oh yes, the poor girl was trembling. She stood amidst shouts of laughter from the other workers."

"Emily, what did your father do?"

"By this time, the workers stopped still and fell silent. They were eager to see what the girl's punishment might be. Father told her she was not alone in her sin, for he knew the temptation the weavers faced every day when they left their cloth and took their wages. After all, their wages are less than the cost to purchase what they had woven in a day. Father called out to the crowd, "Let her among you who never did the like say how this girl should be punished." Nobody spoke. They all quietly began to walk away; so he tossed the cloth to the girl and told her to 'Go, and sin no more.'

"Forgive us our debts, as we forgive our debtors," I added soberly.

"Father says, if we are not forgiven a good deal more than we forgive, we shall all have a hard time of it."

Emily's father is our church organist, so our family has known him for many years. He retained this position even after moving to Lawrence. Now, after hearing this story, I felt I knew his character better. I looked at my friend Emily, as if I knew her character better as well for having shared the story. I was growing quickly more comfortable in confiding in her my dearest thoughts.

"Edward told me some folks in town insisted the Atlantic Cotton Mills could not run without slave labor, but your father has been very successful."

"Oh yes. He was defiant that the workers, mostly Irish immigrants, should—and would—be treated with respect and dignity as free men. Of course, the workers are actually women." Women who were not as fortunate as Emily and I, I thought.

I looked at Emily. She was simply glowing.

"Please tell me more about Mr. Briggs! Are you not a bit apprehensive?"

"No, not at all, and I do not know why. The meeting is perfectly innocent, and I will be free to observe him with others. I am merely invited to tea."

The room was filling with ladies as the church services were long ago ended. Most would convene here for an hour before traveling home. Emily and I interrupted our conversation greeting other parishioners. As quickly as possible, we returned to the topics of utmost importance to us.

Emily asked about Edward, and I explained. "I have not heard from Edward for six weeks. I am arranging travel to Boston in two weeks, so expect to have a good visit."

"What is the last you have heard from him?" she inquired.

"His father is feeling better. Edward has returned to Harvard. His last letter was filled with news of performances by Madam Thillon, Sontag and Alboni."

"Will you attend a concert with Edward when you are in Boston?"

"I hope so. However, I will be accommodating the tastes of traveling companions, so I am not certain what our trip will include. Because we are three ladies, we will more likely join the audience at the Musical Fund than entertain ourselves by dancing! Were Edward to join us, I would enjoy dancing all the more."

We spoke about the most recent soiree at Hamilton Hall. Several others from our church also attend these dances, including Charlie Pierson. I am often in their company. Despite my affection for my cousin, my escorts could be perceived as suitors. Of course, I shall discourage this.

My conversation with Emily is interrupted again, and we graciously respond to inquiries about our health and activities. Back to ourselves, Emily remarks, "There are still so many in society, it seems, who want to have everyone committed to matrimony even years before a lady and man in a couple have determined they have taken a fancy to each other."

I agree. "Well, let us not be the ones to spread further the gossip, which flies about so freely. I suggest we neither defend it nor entertain it."

Emily says I remind her of Edward in this regard. When he was told erroneously of his alleged engagement to Margie Phillips, he chose to merely listen to this shocking tale of fiction. Perhaps, he was right to rise above such baseless speculation. Perhaps, he was right not to respond defensively. Perhaps, he was right not to attack the comment. He has advised me, 'if you wrestle with a pig, you both get dirty, and only the pig has fun.' Such is good counsel for life, albeit a crude concept—wrestling with a pig.

Emily cautions me, "Now, do not reveal too much to your new traveling companions, for you do not know with whom they associate." I had never thought to be cautious in this regard, but I do agree with Emily, it is a prudent approach.

"Do you recall what my brother said about putting on a 'poker face'?" Emily asks me. I conjure up the image of a hot branding poker, with the pig still in my mind. Then, I realize she is referring to a card game often played in the saloons. How does she know about this? Is her brother a poker player? Certainly not Henry! He is a physician. Perhaps she refers to her brother Samuel? Though, he too, seems quite upstanding.

"Lizzie? Do you recall what my brother said?" she asks, bringing my attention back to her.

"Oh, yes, a poker face—to ensure that those around us know nothing of the cards we hold, or the passions of our hearts, before we are ready to expose them," I say, as if I too am suitably knowledgeable about such worldly things.

"Precisely! Though, I must admit to knowing nothing about playing poker," she confesses. "I think card-playing to be a rather vile sort of entertainment. My brother's admonishment, however, gives me a new appreciation that civility can come from such entertainments."

"I see it much like acting in a theatre." I feel perfectly bold in asserting my opinions to Emily, though I was cognizant that *my* opinions were often ones I had heard from others, like my father or Edward! "There is no shame in entertaining an audience, or letting them entertain themselves with their own imaginations!"

Time seems to move most swiftly when I am at tea with Emily.

Other ladies soon begin to gather their wraps before either of us expects the hour has passed. We are the last to depart and walk together to the courtyard where she joins her father and I join mine. They seem not to mind our leisurely pace, for our delay has provided them more time to converse.

On the short carriage ride home from church, the weather is quite cold, although no snow has yet fallen. The sea breeze seems to be frozen in the air, and the horse cuts his way through it. Father is filled with news of the gathering he recently attended in Boston in which plans are being made to honor Mr. Webster next month.

Father insists we hear more about his trip and calls Laura, Joe and me to retire to the parlor. The room is cozy. The chilly weather has warranted a larger fire and the light from the flames reflect throughout the room. My family is together again. Joe being near us every day feels like a delightful enhancement to the conversation. He sees the world unlike any other.

Joe asks Father, "How could Mr. Webster have known so many people so as to draw such a crowd?"

"Before becoming Secretary of State, he was a Senator from Massachusetts and served for fourteen years, nearly all your life, Joe. Your Uncle Tenney knew him quite well." I imagined how the news of Secretary Webster's death must have struck Edward's family, too, what with Senator Tenney ailing also. Father continued, "Both men served as a Senator and a Representative of Massachusetts."

"He was a Senator, a Representative and a Secretary?" Joe inquired.

Father laughs. "Yes, he was, but not all at once. He was among a small number of congressmen initially, but that number has grown. United States Representatives come from every state, and that number is increasing as the population grows. Likewise, the number of Senators is also growing as new states are formed. Just 75 years ago, the U.S. Congress consisted of 13 states. Secretary Webster was instrumental in much of the recent growth and expansion. Now there are 32 states, and each state has men to represent their state's interests. Secretary Webster reminded us that if we are to be 'united' states, we must think of the interests of the country as a whole, not only the needs of our individual states."

"What type of interest do they represent?" I asked. I could imagine the senators listen to gossip at the town hall, but how could they repeat such nonsense in a public forum.

"They establish laws that benefit all the states at the detriment to no others. That is no easy task. There are some states wishing to use slave labor and others insisting on extending our rights of freedom to the slaves. These are serious issues that could divide a country if we cannot learn to compromise."

Father explains, trying as he might to spark our interest. "For example, your dress, Lizzie, most likely started out as cotton on a plantation in South Carolina or Georgia and was picked by slaves before it was shipped to Lawrence to be woven by the mill workers into yardage and cut into a pattern by your dressmaker."

Joe looks at my dress and adds, somewhat absent-mindedly, "Massachusetts does not have plantations. So, our state does not need slaves."

"Correct, yet we need cotton for fabric. Our mills need workers to labor. Some would like to allow slave labor, rather than pay free men to work those same cotton mills." Father gently challenged Joe.

Joe took time for a thoughtful reply. "As far as I have heard, Father, it is women and girls who work in those mills, not men."

"You make an excellent point, Joe. Many of the workers in those mills are the ages of Laura and Lizzie. Their families came to America from Ireland or Canada seeking opportunities to work for wages that would provide food for their families. Many overseers would like to work the girls as if they were indentured servants, but to the girls' good fortune, that is changing today. Some mill superintendents restrict the number of hours a person can work, and do not employ children when there are able-bodied adults they can employ."

Father does not think it a waste of his time to engage us in discussing such matters. I feel nearly obligated to make good use of any knowledge I gain; though, at times, I have little idea how to apply what I know. My own aspirations for teaching may provide the perfect application. Still, I find such knowledge practical, and quite necessary, so that I may hold a conversation of some substance. In fact, Father also encourages me to be knowledgeable about current literature and authors—such as, Dickens, Emerson and Harriet Beecher Stowe, rather than amuse myself only with the stories and fashions of *Godey's Lady's Book.* I am to provide a positive influence on Laura in that regard, as *Godey's Lady's Book* is currently her favorite reading material. I must confess my favorite reading, of course, begins with the words "My dear Lizzie."

United States Currency

Half Cent

Half Dime

Half Dollar

Two and a Half Dollar

CHAPTER 2

Henry and Emily Oliver

Miss M. E. Andrews
Care of Gen. Andrews
Salem
Mass.

Cambridge, [Sunday] Nov. 7, 1852

My dear Lizzie,

I was very much disappointed not to have seen you the Wednesday evening I was in Salem, for I supposed you had moved in from Hamilton long before. Besides your letter told me you would be in Boston the next day and I was anxious to gain your consent to permit me to bring you with Miss Kate P. and Ruth Foster out to Cambridge on Friday or Saturday. But your father told me you had postponed your visit to Boston a fortnight, so I have not yet lost the opportunity of showing you my room.

Be sure and send me word when you will be in Boston and where you will be and that you consent (for you must) to come to Cambridge. I'll show you all connected with the colleges. Joe Brown, Peck, chums, besides Leland, Chase &c.

You can't think how much I was surprised to find your house in Chestnut Street closed. Did Mary Thompson tell you I called? Some one in her house ran to the window when the carriage stopped and I thought 'twas she.

Still I had a very pleasant ride to & from Salem, thanks to Johnny Santos. I took tea at "Grandmother's," called at Aunt Laur's, passed an hour at Carrie Emmerton's, with the Osgoods, who thought I was going to spend the evening at Katy Downing's (of course I wish I had, but I thought it would rain if I staid any longer in Salem.)

If I were going to be in Cambridge all winter I would drive down again in sleighing-time to some Quintette concert and leave Salem about 12, if it were moonlight. But Lancaster (where the young ideas will shoot under my instruction) is too far off to think of such a thing. If I like teaching will try for a school in Danvers next winter and then – oh! think of the concerts, lectures, sleighrides &c. Be careful and not take cold this winter riding after the Quintette concerts.

Daniel Upton called at my room yesterday with Henry Oliver. He will return to Paris in a fortnight.

When I went to Salem George Holyoke seemed very anxious to send some message to Emily Oliver, and by his request I was to imprint a ---- oh! shocking! What an idea! But I didn't see her, and I wish you would deliver his message when you meet Emily. I am going to tell George that Emily is engaged and see what he says to that.

I saw by the Transcript that Clara Putnam has become Mrs. Gadsden. Poor Billy Y., he is "done for life."

Madame Thillon was here last Thursday with Hudson & Mona T.

There will be no Italian opera in Boston this winter (so says rumor) but plenty of concerts. The Germanians begin when the new music hall is ready, the 20th Nov. I believe. I have been to very few rehearsals and afternoon concerts this term though I have nothing to do after dinner but to attend prayers.

You have heard Mlle Lehman in Salem of course. I want very much to come down some evening when the Quintette club has a concert and I was intending to pass a Sabbath with you but it is almost Thanksgiving now. If I see you in Boston I shall know when you will leave Hamilton and perhaps I may go to Salem before I leave college for the term. I have been hoping that Joe would come and pass a day with me and perhaps hear and see Madame Thillon. If he prefers he can return to Salem by the 10½ train.

I suppose you must regret moving to Salem for the winter on account of those morning and evening rides. Have you yet been introduced to T.? I expect to hear of Miss M. L. as having a great passion for early morning walks this winter, very early and usually about the time of the first train from Ipswich. But excuse me, I am trespassing on forbidden ground.

Don't forget to write me when you come to Boston and if it is pleasant I shall bring you out here, s'il vous plait.

My chum would send love if he were here but he is spending the evening with Miss ---?

Good bye till I see you in B.

As ever yr. cousin
E

You may be sure that I will tell you beforehand the next time I visit Salem. All the pleasure of my last call was spoiled by finding that you were in Hamilton for I could not go out there without attracting too much attention.

My school begins the Monday after Thanksgiving & I shall go home the Tuesday before.

Good bye.

I shall expect to have a letter from Joe before Thanksgiving. If by any mishap (which must not occur) you do not come to

Boston, write to me before I leave Cambridge & I will reply from Lancaster.

G. bye.

#That letter is intended for Q but it looks more like a deformed crane.

⸺⸺⸺∽⸺⸺⸺

Tuesday, 9 November 1852

Father picked up the mail and the newspaper. My joyous receipt of Edward's letter was overshadowed by the sad news in the paper about our family. Uncle George has been lost at sea. Father says Uncle George was reported missing from the extreme clipper ship *The Celestial* yesterday. The ship launched from New York in June bound for San Francisco. He arrived there safely in August. Father said he was probably swept overboard on their return. The seas can be turbulent and unruly this time of year. Poor Aunt Laur! They were married in January 1850, and had their daughter Mamie in October 1850. Frankie was born in February 1852, just four months before his father shipped out. Now, little Frankie is only nine months old, Mamie just two years old, and their father is lost! Poor Mamie. Poor little Frankie. How tragic! I felt as if the wind had been squeezed from my lungs. I sat in the parlor for some time as Father broke the news to Aunt Eliza, then to Joe and Laura. I attempted to provide some comfort to Laura, but the day was somber and silent for the most part.

When I retreated to my room at long last, I read Edward's letter and refolded the pages, pressing the cold paper to my bodice, as if I might absorb its contents and every bit of love he poured into it. Oh, that I could only communicate what is in my heart without the trouble of forming words to flow through my pen and fit onto my paper. If only I might hold him. Oh shocking! I would never let him go. A chill ran from my feet to the nape of my neck.

Uncle George's death and the suddenness of Secretary Webster's

40

death left me trembling. How could everything that was once fine in our world be disrupted so quickly? Death changes everything. The little things that once seemed so important are put in perspective with what is truly important. People are all that really matter.

Father acted swiftly to call on Aunt Laur and offer support upon hearing the news of Uncle George. Plans to honor Secretary Webster took longer. As Brigadier General of the Massachusetts Volunteer Militia, Father made arrangements for his unit to join others in Boston on November 30 for a eulogy at Faneuil Hall to honor Secretary Webster. Father is making frequent trips to Boston for this purpose, as well as for his regular business. Lately, Father has seen Edward more than I have. Perhaps he is becoming one of Edward's trusted advisors.

After much consternation, I am prepared to depart in three days to Boston with Father. He invited me, and Joe, to accompany him. We will also meet a ship's captain, who will soon be bringing a large shipment of silk to Salem from the Orient. Thereafter, Joe will return to Salem with Father and I will stay for the week to attend Ruth Foster's wedding. I am to spend the nights in Chelsea with the Fellows and pass my days with Kate Pollard in Boston. Of course, I will savor whatever time I possibly can in Cambridge with Edward. Sunday morning, I will return to Salem for only one week, the week of Thanksgiving. Delavan Mussey is planning to visit us at Thanksgiving in Salem. Our whole family will return to Boston for the eulogy on November 30. With all arrangements confirmed, I let out a sigh of relief. My family's plans had come together just as they should, but one flaw remained—Edward is headed to Methuen for Thanksgiving.

⸺⸺⸺ ⟪⟫ ⸺⸺⸺

❶ General Joseph Andrews' home
38 Chestnut Street
Lived with children and his sister Eliza.

❷ Andrews' Family home
24 Lynde Street
Grandmother Andrews lived with her children Daniel Andrews and Dolly Ann Watkins.

❸ Dr. William Stearns' home
384 Essex Street
Built by Dr. William Stearns Land later bought by Gen. Joseph Andrews.

❹ Grandmother Sprague's home
Corner of Essex and Dean Streets
Occupied by Dr. William Stearns and Sarah White Sprague; then by Joseph E. (Stearns) Sprague.

❺ George and Priscilla Sprague's home
92 Federal Street
Adjoined by home of Rev. Octavius Frothingham

❻ General Henry K. Oliver's home
142 Federal Street
Built by Captain Samuel Cook

❼ Malvina T. Ward home and school
34 Chestnut Street

❽ Rev. James Thompson's home
40 Chestnut Street

❾ Saltonstall Family homes
39 and 43 Chestnut Street

❿ John C. Lee's home
14 Chestnut Street

⓫ Dr. Abel Pierson
Barton Square

⓬ Post Office

⓭ Latin & High School

⓮ Hamilton Hall

N
W
E
S
A MAP OF
SALEM
Residences and Places
1851
ST.
FEDERAL STREET
6
5
CARPENTER ST.
PINE ST.
4
ESSEX STREET
MUNROE
ANDOVER ST.
RIVER ST.
DEAN ST.
8
1
7
3
BECKFORD ST.
FEDERAL ST.
NORTH ST.
GREEN ST.
9
9
CHESTNUT STREET
HAMILTON
CAMBRIDGE
NORTH
UNITARIAN
CHURCH
NORTH RIVER
BROAD STREET
PICKERING ST.
10
SUMMER ST.
2
SEWALL ST.
LYNDE ST.
FEDERAL ST.
BRIDGE ST.
14
CROMBIE ST.
BROAD STREET
CEMETERY
13
11
CITY HALL
MT. VERNON ST.
HIGH ST.
NORMAN ST.
BARTON SQ.
WINTHROP ST.
12
PRATT ST.
MARGIN ST.
R.R.
DEPOT
CENTRAL ST.
ESSEX ST.
WASHINGTON ST.
CENTRAL ST.
CHARTER ST.
DERBY ST.
LAFAYETTE ST.
PEABODY S
HAWTHORNE BLVD.

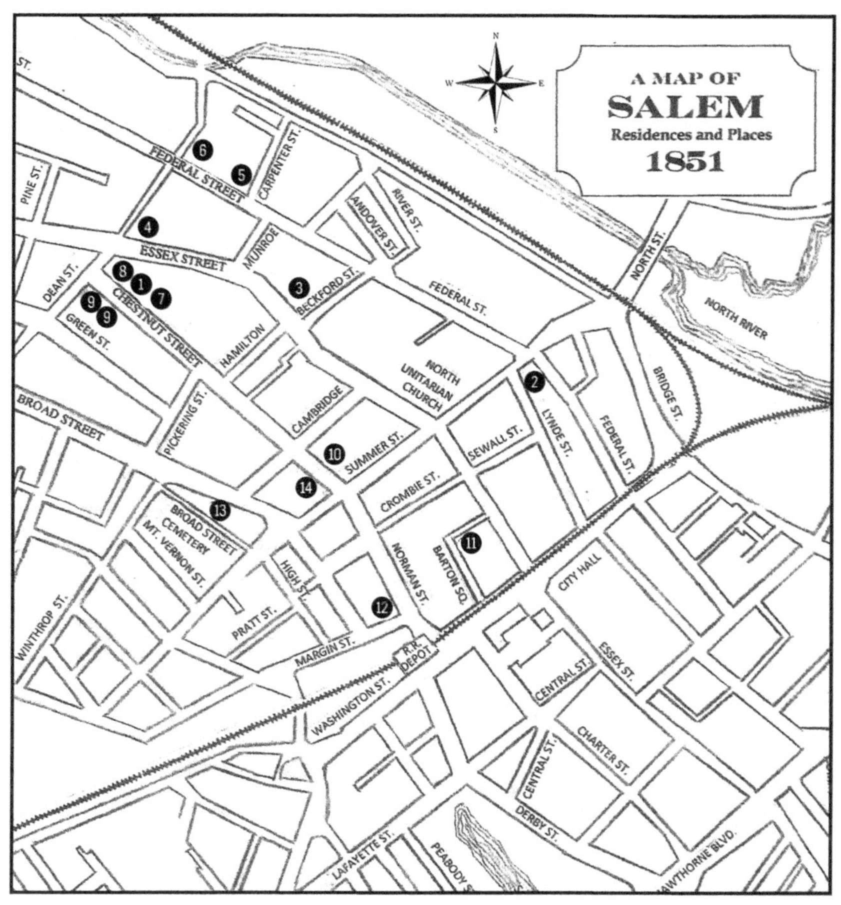

Salem 1851

Thursday, 25 November 1852

My family has a tradition to celebrate Thanksgiving in late November, not on April 13, which is the official Thanksgiving Day declared by the president. Of course, we give thanks on April 13, as we do every day. That day prompts me to begin anticipating my birthday the following week. I am not certain why my extended family observes Thanksgiving as we do. Joe thinks our celebration is 'traditional.' Delavan says it is similar to how families celebrated Thanksgiving in the 1700s. He told us Thanksgiving was once associated with the fall harvest, a time of feasting, often in preparation for fasting. One would reasonably complete their fall harvest and set up foodstuffs by canning vegetables and storing tubers in the root cellar in preparation for a winter without fresh crops.

This year, nine people gathered at the Thanksgiving table—Grandmother, Uncle Daniel, Aunts Dolly and Eliza, Father, my sister, brother and me, joined by cousin Delavan. As we spoke at dinner about all for which we felt thankful, Delavan remarked impersonally and passionately about the rights of women and of slaves and other such talk that had not commonly crossed our dinner table. He was articulate about his beliefs that slaves and also women were able to achieve the same intellectual achievements as white men. I did not doubt the intellectual potential of slaves and women; yet had never given the subject much thought.

Delavan's hair is golden copper, his beard a wiry mass of red. He is more than six feet tall. Laura thinks he looks like a lion. He has a commanding presence, indeed, much like the king of the jungle. His manner of speech has a bit of a roar, though it is not at all unfriendly.

Delavan spoke of his involvement with the Church of New Jerusalem and a man named Emmanuel Swedenborg, of whom I have heard some. I had never met anyone who spoke so eloquently about such new ways of thinking. He inspires me to consider what purpose my life might have, and how I might best prepare to fulfill it.

We settled into the parlor after two hours at table, our Thanksgiving dinners settling inside us. Father and Delavan were the only ones left with anything to say, and while most of us sat in comfort, these two men paced and paraded across the floor. Father inquired of our cousin with an intensity I had not seen before.

"Delavan, how is your father? Has he moved on from teaching medicine at Dartmouth? I heard he is now at Ohio Medical College. Is that right?"

"Yes and no. He has moved already from Ohio to Miami Medical College."

"Do you expect to follow such a path?"

"Of which path do you inquire? The path to Miami or to medicine?"

Father laughed. "Not to Miami, but to the noble profession of medicine."

Delavan paused and then turned half the way around as if to talk to everyone, "Well then, my answer would be…heavens no." He seemed to be putting on a show for someone's benefit, but whose? I could not tell if it was for Joe, Laura, or perhaps me. I only wished it had been Edward center stage once again, but it was not, and my wishing it so would not change a thing. Delevan continued. "There is a long line of physicians in my family, but I, General Andrews, prefer to be a newspaper man."

"A newspaper man?" Father seemed very surprised.

"Absolutely! I agree that there is no more noble a profession than that of a physician. To deliver life into the world and assist in the passing of a human life through stages of infirmity and health to its final conclusion—this must bring a great deal of satisfaction, but it is not the course I choose."

"Pray tell, what in this world could have called you to journalism?" Father asked with an expression that looked like he had bitten a sour lemon.

"I aim to watch life not through a physician's microscope but in another manner altogether. I aim to watch not the simple passing of life, but the drama of life. I aim to follow those who are shaping our times, molding the very world in which we live at the present time. By doing so, I will sculpt history itself by the stories I find and bring to light, recording for all posterity." Delavan looked around the room as he spoke, making eye contact with each person until the other broke the contact, which of course happened immediately with every woman in the room. He passed from Aunt Dolly, to Aunt Eliza, to Grandmother, to Laura. I sat on the other side of Uncle Daniel and Delavan held his gaze for a long time, looking directly at my uncle while speaking in response to Father!

I drew a breath, determined not to be the one to turn when he looked my way. He spun to face Father, not even noticing me!

"I expect I will move out west, perhaps to Chicago or Cincinnati." Delavan continued.

"As a reporter? There are no reporters there, Delavan."

"Exactly, General! There is no one there to objectively record the stories of the pioneers! How will the gentlemen in Boston know what is occurring? How will the senator who must consider the affairs of all the states understand the factors at play in a world so far away from Washington?" Delavan stood quickly and turned suddenly toward me, his red hair flying out around his head as he turned. Laura gasped and, out of the corner of my eye, I could see her draw slightly back in her chair. I lifted my chin and looked directly at Delavan. He looked back. Silently.

"Lizzie, did you say something?" Joe asked.

"No," I answered. I found Delavan to be a most interesting character, but I could not explain my experiment. I wished to see what he would do when faced with a lady who did not look away.

"Delavan, have you a particular interest in politics?" Father drew Delavan's attention from me. I had prevailed, but Delavan, too, had passed the test, yielding only to the authority of General Andrews. Then, Laura flicked her fan with a vengeance and the snap drew me to look at her. Only the General could break Delavan's attention, but I—I fell weak to the crack of a lady's fan.

Sunday, 1 December 1852

I am back in Salem now, filled with reflections of my trip. The eulogy is something I will never forget. Faneuil Hall was dressed to mourn in black draperies with silver letters nearly shouting out at the crowd 'OUR COUNTRY, OUR WHOLE COUNTRY AND NOTHING BUT OUR COUNTRY.' Another drapery panel said, 'LIBERTY & UNION, NOW & FOREVER, ONE AND INSEPARABLE.' About 4,000 persons were present to remember Daniel Webster. Imagine my surprise when I saw my friend Emily Oliver had come from Lawrence and was seated just a few rows in front of us with her father. She caught my eye and gave me a look that seemed to say, 'Once a General's daughter, always a General's daughter.' Truly, Emily and I find ourselves traveling in similar circles. She later chuckled about being one of the Secretary's 1,000 closest relatives. Certainly we all felt like family today.

With 400 present belonging to the cavalcade, another 200-300 arrived in carriages with a grand military escort. The escort consisted of the Boston Brigade and several other companies, including Father's. All other activities in Boston were suspended on that day, November 30. Stores, shops, banks, courts, insurance offices were all closed and all eyes and hearts were united in mourning with Daniel Webster's family and respecting the loss for our country.

I was pleased to have been able to spend time earlier with Edward. We went to a concert in Boston. We read together, walked together and visited with many people he seemed eager for me to meet. However, what I remember most is how he treated me and the feeling that flooded me when he held me in his arms. His chest rose and fell against mine whenever he embraced me and we stole many private moments together in which we simply felt our hearts beat together as one. Shocking! My own heart races at the thought.

Now, I sit at my desk preparing to write. I reach down and dust off my skirts as if they had been somehow tainted by my lascivious imagining. I must thank Edward for his hospitality; thank him for forgiving me my indecisiveness. In person. In Boston. He forgave me for not telling him when I was coming to Boston, and when I was not to come. He forgave me for not coming more often and kissed me, insisting not another word be said about it. Then, he hurried me off to be introduced to his chums. After the fifth or sixth chum, my head was completely spinning. He treated me to dinner and showed me all around Harvard, with more excitement than ever before. He is an upperclassman now and has an air of ownership and pride in his alma mater.

Kate and Edward almost had an opportunity to meet one afternoon in Boston. Edward took me to meet Kate and Ruth, but Kate had been detained and Edward had an engagement so could not delay his departure any longer. He did meet Ruth and, in his own charming way, asked Ruth to thank Kate, on his behalf, for the blackberry charm she once selected for him in New York. The blackberry was a watch fob I had asked Kate to purchase on my behalf as a gift for Edward. He winked at Ruth and assured her he had already thanked me in person. Although an engaged woman, Ruth did not seem to mind his flirtations. Of course, I did not mind either, since he was speaking of me in the kindest of terms.

I am filled with hope for my future and all seems as well as it ever could be in our world. I truly enjoyed my visit with Kate and Ruth, as I expected I would. What I did not expect was how much I enjoyed hearing Father negotiate business. Though the meeting was quick, Father was confident and decisive. The ship captain was exceedingly knowledgeable about the amount of time his journey will take and the risks involved. He requested some investment from Father up front as he wished to share the risks, as is customary. Father was willing to accept some risk, if it resulted in a better price on the silks upon delivery. Although Joe did not appear to be much engaged in listening to the civil banter of the negotiation, this was exciting to me—even more rousing than spending time selecting a few final items to complete a trousseau. Perhaps Joe would have enjoyed the trousseau decisions more. I was honored to share Ruth's excitement about her nuptials and be invited to attend her wedding in Boston yesterday, which was indeed a splendid affair.

--------◦◦◦◦--------

Saturday, 25 December 1852

This month is blowing past me faster than any other December of my remembrance. Our Christmas dinner yesterday at our home had a calm but somber air. There were eight at the Christmas Eve table. Aunt Eliza and Aunt Dolly provided an extraordinary holiday feast featuring roasted turkey with a cranberry sauce, potatoes and beets harvested from Aunt Eliza's garden, along with pickles made from Aunt Eliza's cucumbers. I helped our Irish servants, Margo and Bridget, prepare the sweets to complete the meal. This included mince pies, which we served along with biscuits topped with jellies and jams, and an assortment of nuts. Of course, my aunts and I gave full credit to Margo and Bridget for the perfect preparation.

I made fruitcake all by myself, which Laura and I delivered to each of the neighbors the day before, on little Christmas Eve, December 23. When we arrived at the Pickman's household, we were greeted at the door by Charlie Morris. He is very tall and strong-looking with a most unique face—full lips, a strong jaw and a short, straight nose. His skin tone is very tan, a shade not often seen in the winters of Salem, but not dark enough to look Negro. His eyes are hazel! His broad smile makes his teeth look very white and straight. I found his appearance quite striking, even handsome. His manner of speech did not sound as if he was from Boston at all. I told Laura he might be of mixed race, but she insisted he was just unusual, since no one on Chestnut Street has a Negro servant.

After our deliveries were complete, Joe helped Laura and me decorate the Christmas tree. We popped corn and sat for hours stringing the white puffs between cranberries in a pattern we had seen in *Godey's Lady's Book*. Joe ate so much popcorn he had to cook a second batch to keep up with our 'busy little fingers' as Aunt Eliza called them. As busy as we were, our busy little fingers could not keep up with Joe's busy mouth this day!

The strands were displayed in a draping fashion between the branches. Laura was particularly thrilled to know the berries and corn would later feed the birds when we moved the tree outside behind the house. After the birds had their fill, Edward Clark will cut the tree to become wood for the kitchen cooking stove.

Laura prepared a centerpiece of evergreens that brought the fresh fragrance of the outdoors right inside our dining room. She placed sprigs of holly with red berries around the platter that featured the turkey in the center of the table. Joe mashed the potatoes, a task he seemed to enjoy with a bit too much vocal remonstration for the actual amount of labor involved. Laura rolled her eyes in her head as Joe approached the apple press and prepared to turn the press to extract the apples' sweet juice.

I sat next to Grandmother at the dinner table and she commented that I looked somewhat pale. "Look, Dolly, her complexion is perfectly ashen."

"She looks fine to me, Mother," Dolly reassured her.

"I feel well." I said, but truly something did not feel right with me. I did not have the same excitement and joy I had at Christmases past. Was it because Margo and Bridget had not hung a sprig of mistletoe in the kitchen this year to trap Father's valet? Kitchen mistletoe had almost become one of our Christmas traditions. Perhaps the girls did not want to frighten Edward Clark away so soon, and planned to give him a year to get adjusted.

Grandmother once said I had thin skin and now I believe she could see completely through it–through me! Something was different; something was missing. I examined the red brocade table linens, the silver napkin holders and the silver candlesticks with fresh eyes. These were selected by my mother. How had I not appreciated all that still remained of her influence? For as long as I could remember Mother's large white China platter had sat in the center of the Christmas dinner table with arrangements of fresh fruits, dried figs, berries and nuts of every kind imaginable. That was the only thing I did not see today.

"Where is the fruit?" Laura asked, after dinner.

Father laughed, and all eyes turned to him.

"Have you not filled yourself completely with the meal and the other sweets, Laura?"

"It is not that, Father. I have eaten quite well, but have we no fruit this year? You have always brought us fruit for Christmas."

"And, so I have again. Excuse me." With that, Father retreated and returned carrying a large basket of fruit he had secreted in the parlor. The familiar, yet exotic, treats for which we yearned were piled one upon the other until the basket was filled to the brim. Father carried the basket around the table and we selected a treat, including pieces of chocolate. It was all there and I saw in an instant how he had been filling in for all that was missing since the loss of our mother. Never before had I appreciated his efforts, or the joy that it seemed to bring him. I imagined the day I could build such fine traditions for my husband and my children. I saw Edward in my picture and longed to engage in a vigorous reflection with him of all that has passed since last Christmas. It was more than fruit that was missing for me this Christmas. I felt a flush of heat at the thought and tossed my head to clear the silly rumination.

"Well, Mother, it seems Lizzie merely needed a bite of fruit to bring the color back into her face," Aunt Dolly declared.

Joe loudly slurped the juice from his orange, completely unaware of anyone's conversation. "Are you enjoying the orange, Joe?" Aunt Dolly laughed.

"Mmmm-umm." Joe's reply lightened the mood, and no one noticed that my thoughts—not the fruit—had stirred a blush in me that raced enough color to my face to match my crimson dress!

After dinner everyone retired to the living room to gather around the Christmas tree. Three gifts hung from the tree. Laura looked at me when she saw them and whispered, "Lizzie, are those for us and Joe?"

"I suppose so." I whispered back.

Father took the packages from the tree and handed them to his brother and sisters. Laura and I exchanged a glance. I could see her confusion, but Joe sat smiling on the sofa, seeming not at all surprised.

Dolly was the first to speak to my father. "Joseph, whatever have you done?"

Aunt Eliza gave Father a sweet peck on the cheek and appeared to whisper something into his ear.

"Thank you, little brother," was Uncle Daniel's response, which provoked a giggle from Laura. It was a perfectly respectable remark, for Uncle Daniel was quite a bit older than my father. Still, we had never heard him, or anyone, refer to Father as such. Quite frankly, the thought that our father was a 'little' brother seemed particularly amusing to me on this day, one in which I had spent entirely too much time mired in absurd imaginings of abandonment by those I love. We were all here and each was well and my father was surrounded by hearty elders.

I imagined my father with his sisters and brother as children— Father and Dolly, just two years apart, cared for by Eliza and Daniel. Father told me there was another Joseph before him, the fourth child of seven, but he died as an infant. Father was given that name to carry forward to the next generation.

Soon Laura was on her feet, whispering something to Grandmother, who laughed and then spoke loudly, "Yes, my dear, the children will have gifts this year, unless you think you are not deserving."

Laura looked at me for confirmation. My brother jumped up from his seat, and announced, "I will get Laura's gift." He departed toward the kitchen. Aunt Dolly followed. They returned with four large boxes wrapped in silk cloth and tied with long ribbons. Dolly handed one package to Grandmother while Joe stood, arms filled with the others. The top box went to Laura. She began to bounce in her chair with excitement. The next, a round box went to me. Joe stood with the final package. Dolly instructed him to sit down, saying, "That one is for you."

We each sat with a gift in hand…except Father. I suddenly felt heartsick, for he had nothing. How could Father have been forgotten?

We sat patiently, waiting for what I did not know. Then, Daniel walked across the room, and handed Father a small velvet bag. He said, "Happiest of Christmases to you, dear brother." Then, the joy could be felt.

Dolly spoke to Grandmother, "Open your box first, Mother." She had fashioned a new cap for Grandmother to wear in the house. "I know you prefer to wear a cap most days," she said. She glanced toward me as she continued to speak, "although such attire is beginning to lose favor with today's young women."

"Oh, p'shaw, what do they know!" Grandmother replied. "This is lovely, Dolly; perfectly lovely!"

As was our custom, we opened gifts one at a time. Laura was next. She untied the ribbon and handed it to Grandmother, along with the silk that enclosed the box and made its appearance so festive and grand. While Grandmother carefully folded the silk, Laura presented for all to see her new porcelain doll. It was not one for a child, however, being much too delicate for childish play. Rather, this doll would be displayed in her room to be admired. Grandmother fashioned the clothing, Dolly the hat, and Joe, of all people, had painted the face! It was not the first he had done, either. Father says I am to keep that a secret from anyone other than family. Regardless, Joe is quite proud of his creation!

Joe opened his gift next. Grandmother selected for him a fine black merino wool for a new waistcoat. The tailor began its construction without Joe's knowledge, based on an old coat he acquired at Somerville. Although it was unfinished, he looked very striking in his new frock. He did not express a speck of gratitude, however; not even a smile. I felt ashamed for him. Clearly, he received more pleasure from seeing the doll he had helped fashion than he did from receiving a gift.

My aunts and uncle opened their gifts to discover Father had purchased broaches for his sisters and a new watch chain for his brother. I wondered if Kate Pollard had helped him select these gifts for the chain had a beautiful charm, which looked much like a tiny pine cone. Daniel, in turn, gave Father a silver money clip engraved with his initials JAA.

For me, Aunt Dolly fashioned a bonnet. It is the most marvelous I have seen for a young lady. It fits perfectly just above my hair, which I pull back into a knot at the nape of my neck. She called it a spoon bonnet because it rises above my forehead with a curve and slopes at the back. It has but a tiny brim above my ears and wide ribbons for bonnet strings, which of course I will not crush by tying, but will clasp them together with a pin. The ribbon is blue silk. Aunt Dolly says I may use her old broach to fasten them.

"Thank goodness, you did not fit the child with an ugly," said Grandmother.

"What in heaven's name is an ugly?" I asked, never having heard of such a thing. Dolly explained. "It is a bonnet with an extra brim of cane covered with silk. It is practical for keeping away the sun, but I must agree with Mother, that it is not the most fashionable."

We spent the rest of the evening singing Christmas Carols. For some reason, Laura and I have been relegated the honor of selecting the songs and leading the singing. We do not mind, of course. Laura is always eager to sing, and her sweet voice is a joy to hear even if one does not wish to sing along. Joe often does not, but Father and Grandmother have exceptional voices for singing.

CHAPTER 3

Death's Scourge

Miss M. E. Andrews
Care of Gen. J. Andrews
Salem
Mass.

Methuen, [Saturday] Dec. 25th 1852

Dear Lizzie,

If I had not been called away from college last month I might have passed today in Salem or at least driven down for a few hours on Christmas eve. But of course everything is for the best and I am thankful that I can be of some service anywhere.

I sit up with Father a part of every night and that is the only time I find for writing, as I am employed all day long. Now don't retort upon me for laughing at your excuse of "no time" for I am really busy: and besides I promise to be perfectly contented if you will send very often each letter as your last. I was so much delighted by those three well-filled pages that I would have replied that very night of their reception in hopes of getting a Second Edition, but for an aged friend of mine, Dame Prudence. Now cara cuj- you must never decrease the length of your letters to me.

Did Delavan Mussey visit Salem at Thanksgiving? I was very anxious that he should do so, and wait upon Lucy Osgood, and you of course, if you were envious of the distinction, to the Quintette concert, lyceum or some other public place.

Mother thought that Delavan was crazy and even Liz acknowledged that he had grown somewhat plain. He seemed very much smitten ("Smashed" dit-on) and acted before all quite as silly as a certain other young gentleman (modesty?) used to do. I was particularly anxious that Lucy O. should have the pleasure of D's society, for she is particularly fond of his attention.

I can't tell when I may accept your kind invitation to meet Kate Pollard in Salem, for I should not leave home for a whole day while father remains as he now is. He has thought for a week past that he would recover, but his disease is so variable and so flattening that but little confidence is to be placed in favorable symptoms.

When he sent for me to return home in November, he thought that any day might be his last. Soon after I came home, he said to me "Edward, I want to have a few moments conversation with you, for I may never see you again." He said this in expectation that I would return to Cambridge that day to continue my studies. Then he talked with me as he had done before with Liz and Mary, and I thought it might be the last time I should ever converse with my father. He told me what he would have me do when he were gone and my mother and sisters would have no one to assist them save myself. He explained wherein I should change to supply his place and be as well as I could the head for the rest to look up to with confidence. Though I tried hard to talk calmly with him, yet something made the tears flow against my will: for I felt how unprepared and unfit I was to take my father's place, and how much I had neglected to train myself for such a crisis. How much would I have given for an older brother!

Oh! Lizzie. No family is secure from Death's scourge. Have you ever thought that you might be left an orphan at any time? Who can say that you will have a father one year from hence? It is sad to talk and think thus, but since I came home, everything like this has been brought forcibly to mind, and I have, more than once, reflected how very sad would be your bereavement should your father sicken and die. With no brother in whom you can feel that perfect confidence you would have, you would be but ill-prepared to meet alone the rough world and buffet every wave of adversity.

I wish that I could see you now and talk with you as I feel, for if ever one needs a friend ready to sympathize with himself, it is when fearing bereavement.

Father has just waked and wishes me to retire now. If I could only go back to the last night of your visit here last summer! Good night. I must add a word more tomorrow.

Affectionately yrs
Edward -

Sunday P.M. Wilson has my school in Lancaster and he writes me that he has a fine time, keeping singing-school in addition to the other. I wanted to bring you out to our room very much when I was in Cambridge.

Sister Liz has been propounded for admission to our church, and will probably join in January. I shall write to Joe very soon. I wish that he could be such a brother as you would have him to be?

There is a very pretty young lady staying at the Davises' this winter, and if I were not busy at home I should be tempted to call on Miss J. Davis very often.

Several of my friends have congratulated me on my engagement with Margie Phillips. Rather good that. Of course

I don't deny it, but shall ask Margie's advice for an answer. Oh! shocking -

Sister Margie has been at Mrs. Cabot's nearly a month.

Don't you want Lottie? If so write up soon, immediately. Three pages, at least. Of course you can't have her, but then do send for her through me -

If Miss Felt asks for father, tell her he is much better than when she was here.

Good bye –

Yr. Cousin E-
Do write soon.

⸙

Friday, 31 December 1852

Yesterday I read Edward's letter over and over again when I should have been preparing for our New Year's celebration. How can we celebrate when Edward has said his father is near death? He evoked such sad sentiments in me. Whereas time passes gradually for him as he composes a portion of his letter throughout his day, time collapses all he experiences into a single hour as I read, being tossed and turned a dozen times.

I am struck by a wave of great sorrow for his loss and too soon flooded with jealousy. Friends congratulate him on his engagement with Margie Phillips. Shocking! Why does he not deny such an atrocity outright? Rather, he seems amused. No one suspects he has any *other* love-interest besides Margie. Suspicion about Margie is not amusing to me in the least. Her 'engagement' does not put me in a mind to celebrate! Yet, the New Year is upon us and, like Margie, cannot be stopped from advancing!

Though the coming of 1853 is certainly good reason to rejoice, I could not help but retreat to my room overcome with deep grief, or was this simply childish fear I feel?

Like Laura, I have *indeed* feared I might be left an orphan, and I wept as if my own father were dying with a sense of loss that seemed to

58

have no end. I buried my face in my feather pillow and let my tears soak the linen clear through. I could smell the dampened goose down. The memory of that scent only made it worse for I do not think I have cried as much since my mother passed on.

Oh, Edward! Why am I not at your side just now?

My mother has been so long gone and my father is too often away. No one can say that any of us might not suffer a tragic loss one year from hence! As I wept, I wondered about the worst imaginable circumstance in which I might find myself. My father could fall ill. My brother could return to Somerville or go to sea and be lost. Grandmother surely shall not live forever. Aunts Dolly and Eliza could marry and leave this home, and of course we would bless their happiness, but how might we carry on without Aunt Eliza? Uncle Daniel and I would be left to care for Laura. Oh, heavens!

My mind would not stop until I imagined every conceivable drama and had run it through its full course. When I reached its finale, I felt ashamed for allowing myself such a morbid indulgence for I realize the entire absurdity of my situation. Here in my room I was crying that I might lose my father, yet downstairs at that very moment, he sat—alive and well.

I pulled myself from the bed and poured a splash of water into my wash basin. After wetting my face with it, I felt I had not a moment to waste in joining my dear family downstairs and rushed out of my room. Flying down the stairs, I found Father standing by the fire in the library. He held a fire poker. The book he was reading lay open on the nearby chair. A steaming cup of tea sat on the table by the kerosene lamp. Hearing me, he turned his back to the fire to face me. I threw my arms around him and clung as if I were still a small child.

"Lizzie, what is the matter? Lizzie?" He spoke slowly, his voice soothing but concerned.

I held tight, pinning his arms to his sides, and buried my head in his chest. He still held the poker. He grasped my arm with his free hand, and pushed me gently away to look into my face.

"Tell me, Lizzie. What is it?"

I spoke to his chest for my eyes would surely expose my childish behavior. I burst out, "I love you, Father."

"My dear girl, is that a matter for such sadness?"

"I am no longer sad, Father, but I am entirely absurd! I did cry, but my tears have dried." I wiped my cheek to make sure no trace was left, though I imagined my eyes reflected all the sorrow that had passed from them into my pillow feathers. "Those tears were shed when I thought, I thought…Oh, Father, I never want to lose you!"

"Lizzie, you silly, silly girl."

Father and I talked all afternoon about Edward's letter, and his father. We talked as we had never done before. By the time the family gathered around for supper, I felt quite prepared to greet a new year. The chimes on the clock kept track of our journey through time but only Father and I remained awake to hear the succession of twelve chimes that marked the beginning of the New Year.

***

Saturday, 1 January 1853

By the time I arose, the house was filled with activity. Grandmother and Dolly had already arrived as I made my way down the stairs. I glimpsed an array of papers, ink bottles and pens scattered all about the dining room table. In the parlor across the foyer, I could hear Grandmother speaking, "Clearly, there are some to whom a good stiff discourse is in order. I, for one, am not about to tip-toe around my grandson for fear he will fly into a rage. I suppose it would be my place to see to it that he receives his due, and if Somerville is again in his future, then let it be."

I entered the parlor where Dolly sat, diligently stitching beads to netting that draped a black satin hat, most likely for a period of mourning. She did not say a word. Dolly wore a slight smile frozen, but not to express her feeling. Three hatpins jutted from between her lips. She plucked the pins, one at a time. They quickly reappeared on the hat as the parade of beads marched across the netting.

"Who would be in need of a discourse from you, Grandmother?" I asked. "My brother, perhaps?" She has been intent on helping Joe find his purpose in life, ever since he returned from Somerville—and especially over the holiday, when we spend so much time together as a family. She encourages any useful vocation—his painting doll faces or doing fancywork would please her. Joe, however, knows such female activity concerns Father, and so, Joe remains at an impasse. He seems not a bit concerned with the necessity to engage in *any* occupation. He simply has no plans that would provide a livelihood for himself, let alone for his family. He appears to be content to idle his time away sketching.

Grandmother was quick to respond to my inquiry. "This is not a matter for your concern, Mary Elizabeth," she scolded me, but then warmed to divert my attention. "Have you seen such work as the type your Aunt Dolly is doing?"

"Not closely, and…" I barely began my response when Grandmother pushed against the arms of her chair to bring herself upright, and rose to leave the room.

I stopped speaking. Aunt Dolly looked up at me, eyed Grandmother and, with a shrug, returned to her work.

Joe had entered the house and Grandmother met him in the foyer.

"Where have you been, young man?" Grandmother confronted him.

"Out for a walk."

"Joe, you spread your belongings all about and left without a word. Look at that dreadful, unsightly mess." I could see her wagging her finger toward the dining room. "Whom did you expect would contend with your mess in your absence?" She paused only slightly, not allowing time for a thoughtful response and then continued. "Due to your carelessness, no one else could use the dining room." This having little impact on Joe, she added, "Aunt Dolly was not able to engage in her millinery work as she had planned."

Grandmother stood solid on her feet; hands on hips, her head tilted upwards so as to look Joe in the eyes. Her back was quite straight for one her age and there was nothing feeble about her delivery, though it was clear she could not hear my brother's response very well. Nor could I. His head gradually fell forward as Grandmother spoke. Joe's eyes never left the floor.

"Have you nothing to say?" She asked.

He mumbled a response, but what left his mouth was not decipherable as words. Then he shuffled quickly backward out of the room, knowing better than to turn his back on Grandmother. She simply shook her head and I heard her exclaim, "Good Lord!" as if in a cry for help. I was shocked to hear her voice such an oath. Certainly, she must have meant it in prayer. I silently joined her prayer that the good Lord would do something for Joe.

CHAPTER 4

The Patient Waiter Is No Loser

Miss M. E. Andrews
Care of Jos. Andrews Esq.
Salem
Mass.

Methuen, [Sunday] February 6th 1853

Dear Lizzie-

It is not often that toothache is welcome: but last month toothache almost drove me to Salem for relief, and therefore for once this nervous guest was welcome. But this is the greatest progress Salem-ward that I have made for a long time. I begin to think I shall stay in the country like Rip Van Winkle till the great grandchildren of my Salem acquaintances stare at the old grey-beard visiting their city after an absence of ___(?) years. But I say to myself as "Cousin Sally" used to tell Johnny when he teased for cake "the patient waiter is no loser."

Now if there was only some young lady in whom I had as much interest as you have in "Charlie," I might imitate your example and give some extracts from Wilson's letters or from Johnny Santos (for he has written me once.)

Your cousin, Delavan Mussey, came here at half past ten last Wednesday evening and went away the next morning before the family was up. He told me he did not visit Salem at Christmas.

Gallants in Methuen are so scarce that the young ladies have to adopt most extraordinary measures to secure attention. Margie Phillips came home for New Years day and one evening had eight or ten girls to take tea &c. The night was dark as pitch and with a lantern I called for Liz & Mary. Up started the whole crowd and as they came out with M. & L. I had to trot all over town dropping one at a time till I reached home. The same thing occurred a few evenings afterward and at last I told Liz I shouldn't call for her in future. Very brotherly that, but I was as cross as a bear.

You call Whittemore handsome, but I hope his style of beauty is different from Charlie M's.

I should be greatly obliged to Miss Pollard for another blackberry, but I shan't surrender this one till I see the second of course. You see how shrewd and cunning I have grown since I turned lawyer. I am requested to deliver a lecture on Temperance: would you accept? Admittance free!

I haven't seen Emily Oliver since I left college. Does she go to Salem daily? If so, why won't you come up in the cars with her some day and I will bring you to Methuen. I was going to propose to Joe, if we had sleighing, to drive you up some day. But do, if you can, ride up with E. some time.

I met James Gillis in Lawrence in December when at concert sitting nearby and was introduced by Mrs. Cabot. He appears finely and looks ditto. Mrs. C. told me afterwards that he was a most perfect Son.

But father says "I shan't need you any more," so Good-night-

7th   Father is sleeping and I have the whole evening to write. I was compelled to close very abruptly last night, for the least delay in compliance with father's wishes disturbs him, and when he says I may go, he is fidgety till I do go.

Why is it that I can't write a decent letter to you? When I read over what I send you I find that I have a mass of stuff either most insufferably spooney or awful silly. But "live and learn" is the motto for all, both wits and fools, and therefore with apology and regret for the past I shall try to mend, one of these days.

Joe owes me a letter which I shall expect very soon. I was glad to hear from your father that he seemed so well this winter and was apparently happy and contented.

From JW I only hear occasionally and I know not where he spends his vacation. Carrie I see once in a while, also Sarah White.

Be sure and come up with Emily O. if you possibly can. I heard of your being at Papanti's hall, but I didn't see you.

You won't cry over this letter I know, even if you have patience to read the whole. Excuse me this once and I promise better.

Do write as soon as you can, and have no fear of writing too much. The last two letters are perfect almost and I would gladly repay you if I could.

I would of course, have visited Salem long before this, if I could but father would be unwilling to have me away unless plea of absolute necessity.

Good bye — write very soon
E.
"Much love to all" Very much. Good bye.

Saturday, 26 February 1853

Upon receipt of Edward's letter, I pondered the news about JW, Carrie and Sarah White, and his comments about Emily, Charlie and

Whittemore. JW and Joe previously spent quite a bit of time together discussing inventions and innovations, drawing designs for ships and trains with steam engines. I do not believe Joe has seen JW since he graduated from Harvard.

As for Cousin Carrie, she must be very fond of Edward, having spent time with him when he attended Quaboag Seminary in Warren, Massachusetts. She and her husband, the Rev. Charles Smith, are well-situated in Warren to rear their two young children.

Cousin Sarah White Sprague is 60 years old and unmarried. She is quite attentive to keeping family members, those who are less able to travel, informed about other family members. Do not think I am calling her a busy-body or a gossip! Not at all. She is a dear, and a joy to visit.

I often see Emily at the train station in Salem waiting for the train to Lawrence. I suggested to her that Edward would be an aptly competent orator. I expect his speech would be well-composed and his delivery would be dramatic. She told me her father planned to ask Edward to give such a speech in Lawrence at the mills. With his lawyerly demeanor, he would surely compel the ladies to listen. The working girls would absolutely swoon to hear such a handsome esquire express sympathy for their plight, especially since they would meet him as someone not yet promised to anyone. Emily offered to make all the particular arrangements.

Now that I have instigated such an arrangement, I am not sure I entirely approve of my own idea! Why expose Edward to so many adoring young ladies, especially if I am not present!

Emily's eldest brother, Samuel, works at the mill as a clerk. She tells me he has no shortage of attention from the ladies working in the mills. As an officer in the Massachusetts Volunteer Militia regiment, which he organized in Lawrence, the girls swoon over the handsome Captain Oliver. Emily says if she were a betting woman, she would place a wager that her brother Samuel will be married within the year. Of course, she is not—nor am I—so no wager is placed between the two of us! Mercy me, how does Emily even come up with such ideas?

Perhaps I can ride with Emily to Lawrence to hear Edward's speech on temperance! If he could pick us up, we promise not to bring all our girl friends to be dropped off at their homes! I dare say Margie Phillips takes great advantage of his chivalry.

How does Edward come up with ideas about my interest in Charlie Morris? He is a servant, albeit a very handsome one! Perhaps he will share a recipe with me, or provide me a cooking lesson. Certainly, Grandmother would approve, as it would build my self-sufficiency!

Now William Henry Whittemore is another story! Edward should be jealous for if Whittemore were closer than Cambridge, I would delight in dancing with him more often. He is most interesting, although tales of his adventures frighten me. He told me of his steamer ship striking a rock near Owl's Head in Maine imperiling the lives of those on board. That he was young and strong allowed him to not only save himself but assist other passengers to safety. He was most modest in his telling this tale, but quite animated in discussing his other travels, including his winter break in Washington where he became acquainted with many elected officials. Whittemore has extravagant plans for exotic travel in the future and I have no doubt he will accomplish all he sets out to do.

Saturday, 2 April 1853

I settled into the parlor after supper arranging my embroidery across my lap, selecting several strands of green thread to use on a flower leaf I had drawn on a remnant of light-colored linen. Father entered with his book and settled in his armchair situated on the other side of the window. We often sat silently, side by side in front of the window, separated by only a small table with a kerosene lamp. When day's light faded, the lamp lit our books and my handiwork. Today, I did not choose silence.

"Father, may I travel to Lawrence to hear Edward provide an oration at the textile mill on the subject of temperance?"

"Why not invite him here to speak of such matters in our own parlor?" Father simply does not understand the situation I am facing. I wish so much to have a visit with Edward. I fear a rendezvous of any sort appears impossible at this time.

"Edward has been very busy attending to his father. He is at his father's bedside every day."

"True, his father's health is waning of late." That was all Father said. Certainly, Father realizes how ill Uncle John is. By God's own will, he rallies only to weaken again. He seems to have no control over his situation, as Edward has none over his and I seem to have none over mine. What part does his 'free will' play in this? Surely God's will surpasses the free will of man in matters of life and death. My sympathy for his situation makes me want to see him that much more, not entirely for my own benefit. If he has forgotten me, my appearance would remind him of something other than the imminent passing of his beloved father. Perhaps this will stir in him the resolution to make a plan for his life and future. Does he not see how I would fit with such a plan? Is it terribly selfish of me to appeal to God for assistance in matters of the heart?

"You can certainly extend an invitation," Father said and with that I knew the subject was closed. I will write and at least express my regrets and my sincere desire to have attended.

Edward driving his sister's friends home

CHAPTER 5

Should Not Fear to Die

Miss M. E. Andrews -
Care of Gen. J. Andrews
Salem
Msette.

Methuen – [Tuesday] 12th April [1853]

Dear Lizzie-

When I left the bedside of my dear father last Friday night, and mother clung so closely to me with a feeling of loneliness that seemed overpowering to her I felt that I would have given the world for one hour of your society. I restrained my grief for mother's sake, yet when I was alone it seemed a great relief to cry and I know what comfort it must be to weep with a sympathizing friend. Oh Lizzie, had you been here I could have been as calm to the world as a stranger who had not lost his best friend.

I hope that you may long be spared such a bereavement.

Expectation is nothing: for though one may have been months awaiting death almost hourly, yet when it does come and the apparently agonizing struggles, those dreadful gaspings for breath and then the still calm form announce that Death is come, the feeling must be the same as if the departure were sudden and unexpected.

Now, it is a pleasure to talk with mother of father, and call to mind every incident connected with him. There seems nothing gloomy about his death and no shuddering when we touch his cold, clammy brow.

I should not fear to die any time. All father's suffering must be ended, he must be in a happier world and why should we dread to meet him there? When the face that by its sweet, calm expression tells us that father must be well, is hidden in the dismal tomb, perhaps the mourning may be far from comforting, but now, I could not wish him back again to lie on that sick bed through another day of pain.

Dear Lizzie, if you could come to Methuen next Friday, it would be very gratifying to me.

Do try and be here unless you do not wish to. I feel as if I could not be easy without you.

Good bye till I see you.
Edward
I shall write you again soon

Wednesday, 13 April 1853

Today is declared to be the Federal day of Thanksgiving, but I am glad we are not planning a family celebration. Instead, we are mourning our loss of Uncle John Tenney, who died on Friday, the 8th of April. Loss does not lend one to feel thankful. Edward says his father's passing was peaceful and now he himself no longer fears dying at any time. Edward's uncle, William Jarvis Cutts, also passed away last week. I silently counted the number of women and girls who have depended on the two late uncles to see to their well-being. None of this leads one to feel thankful.

⸺⟡⸺

Sunday, 17 April 1852

On the third Sabbath in April, Father drove Joe, Laura and me in the carriage to Methuen to pay our respects to Edward's family. There was a great deal of grief and the fear among the family members was visceral. Edward greeted us at the door—Father first, then Laura. Father and Laura continued into the house. I wanted to throw my arms around him, comfort him, but he gave me the same obligatory peck on the cheek as he had offered my sister; though I pressed close to him and looked up into his face. His eyes met mine ever so briefly. I was the one who needed comforting.

"Thank you for coming, Lizzie." Edward's voice was quiet and calm.

"Oh, Edward…" The rest of my words lodged under the lump in my throat.

The voices behind me prompted me to move into the house and I entered a sea of somber faces and women in black. The youngest children were the only animated figures in the Tenney home that day. Johnny, now eleven, tried his best to watch out for little sisters Lottie and Maggie, I mean Jimmie, as others call her these days. I simply cannot remember to call sweet little Lottie "Jimmie." No one minded, or perhaps even noticed.

After Joe entered, and paid his respects very briefly, he gathered the children and moved them into the formal dining room, away from all the mourners in the rest of the house. Soon the laughter of little children could be heard in the distance. No one could discourage such a thing, although no one else would have thought to deem it appropriate.

With the children duly occupied, Aunt Augusta seemed free to mourn. She kept a tight grasp on the bodice of her dress, as if she were shielding her heart. She opened her arms to me as I approached her.

"Oh, Aunt Augusta," I blurted and stepped into her arms, feeling her sob. I could not hold back my own tears. I felt so much loss, as if

Joe plays with the children

I too were alone in the world with no one to return my love. Behind her, Uncle John was laid out in the parlor among so many early spring flowers and fragrant Easter lilies. Edward stood close by his side, and remained there most of the day. I tried to catch his eye but to little avail. He could not see beyond his duties. Men streamed in to speak with him about his father's contributions to the state of Massachusetts and the town of Methuen.

Edward was stoic. He hardly looked in my direction. I cannot bare the agony of his rejecting the tenderest feelings I have ever known for anyone at any time. Why is it that I am oft pursued by ones in which I have little interest, while I cannot turn the eye of the only one who holds my heart?

Must I accept that with so much responsibility now, there is no future for Edward and me together? Must I accept that he does not care for me in the same manner as I do him? Must I surrender gracefully to my fate to spend my life with him as never anything more than a dear cousin? I pray that he will find some time for me and I shall retain a piece of his heart.

Saturday, 23 April 1853

Although I have been quite busy with school, family and social engagements, I think of nothing but Edward! That which we feared truly has come to pass. Edward is alone in the world with no father on this earth to guide him. How immensely lonely such an existence must be. Had it been my own father who had taken to the grave, I might have followed him, for I could not bear to watch my life change in the dreadful ways I expect it would following such a loss. As a man, Edward has not been struck with that type of dread. His is an altogether different terror. He must be strong—for his mother and siblings depend on him now, just as his father forewarned. I only wish I could be more supportive during this time. There is simply not an appropriate way in which to do so, for I have not received a word from him since his father's passing.

Friday, 13 May 1853

I leave the post office empty-handed and continue on my way down Chestnut Street. Edward has not written in nearly a month. I hoped to receive at least a bit of his attention by now. It need not be a heartfelt missive of his intentions toward me. I would welcome a short note about how he is faring after his father's passing. Hearing nothing, I fear he has been finding comfort during this difficult time from other people. If my suspicions are correct, he has turned his attention to someone other. Oh, dread!

I look up and seek something about the spring day that might successfully distract me from my thoughts. I see a young lady across the street being escorted by a gentleman. Does she look a bit like Margie Phillips? No, I do not know either of them. I nod to acknowledge I have seen them, just in case they noticed me. Clearly, they have not; their attentions seem to be focused only on each other. I feel forgotten and invisible. I expect to hear news soon of Edward's engagement. I suspect he will wed Margie Phillips. Perhaps he is destined to become a minister, and as such he should marry Reverend Phillips' daughter. I simply may not be the one for Edward. I try to prepare myself. Someone other will surely cherish me some day, for no other reason than they could marry a successful merchant's daughter.

I have accepted an invitation to a tea dance with Whittemore—I recently suggested Edward look for him and tell me what he thinks. This is not a ploy to make him jealous, very much, well perhaps a bit. Whittemore and I get on finely, but my heart sits still and heavy when I cannot see my cousin. I must force my heart to follow my head. There is no reason to refuse an invitation for dancing with Whittemore or Charlie Pierson; although I have not seen Charlie of late.

Shocking! Just as I thought of Charlie Pierson, Father told me the tragic news that Charlie's father, Dr. Abel Pierson, died in a tragic railroad accident, along with 48 people. Six other physicians, who were returning home from the Sixth Annual Meeting of the American Medical Convention, also died. There has never been a railroad disaster of this magnitude. The train engineer simply did not see the open drawbridge, through which a steamship has just passed. He was a substitute driver. He could not stop the train before it plunged into the harbor. Dr. Pierson was Senator Tenney's doctor. Charlie is a chum of Edward's from Harvard, and a friend of Joe's and mine. Charlie lost his sister Harriet and his twin brother James just six years ago and now has lost his father.

Norwalk rail disaster

CHAPTER 6

Give up my Profession

Miss M. E. Andrews
Care of Gen. J. Andrews
Salem
Ma

Methuen, [Sunday] May 22d /53.

My dear Lizzie-

You must excuse, for this time, my month's delay in writing you; for I have been waiting till I could tell you what I had decided to do; but now I am no more decided than I was a month since. I have felt it a duty to give up my profession "under existing circumstances," and of course have been somewhat impatient to be in some business rather than idling away my time at home.

What I engage in will depend upon the receipt of news from New York, which I have been expecting for some time. As yet I have told no one, except Mother and two or three gentlemen whose advice I asked, what my plans are for they may have to be changed, and I don't want to have any appearance of indecision.

I have not yet rejoined my class in college because, to do that, I should have to pass an examination in the studies omitted the past six months. The faculty will probably grant me my degree, when the class graduates. For two weeks I have been to Boston every day to study Book-keeping, etc. and this will occupy me some time yet. I see Emily Oliver quite often in the cars, between Boston and Lawrence; she has a vacation now for a short time.

Liz spent a few days in Boston last week, we heard Sontag in Don Giovanni Monday eve. I wished you had been there, to have enjoyed the music and acting as we did. We were late for the Chelsea ferry boat and rode over in a rickety cab.

I wish you would come to Boston soon, if you can. The rehearsals are over, but an excuse can easily be found for a day or two. "Spring shopping?" Won't that do? If you will send me word when and where I can meet you some day, I will tell you more fully what I am going to do. I intended to have passed a few days in Hamilton this summer and I still hope to be able to, but not for a few weeks, at least.

Do you ride horse-back yet? If not you must begin soon. You will be sure to enjoy yourself. I expect to go out riding with you in Hamilton, and if you should disappoint me, I fear I should put you on "Major's" back by main strength as the first lesson.

I was at Cambridge last week but I did not see Whittemore. I hope to meet him "Inauguration day." (Tuesday)

Liz says she is going to spend a part of the Summer in Maine with an uncle, who has plenty of young horses etc. etc. She anticipates "a splendid time."

Since January last I have written to no one but you and Joe (except business letters) so that I may ask you to not "view me with a critic's eye" either in style, penmanship or punctuality.

Sunday is the only time I have for writing, as I am in Boston all day, and busy in the evening till bed-time. If I sit up late I miss the morning cars. I hope to hear from you very soon - a good long letter - Good bye -

Yrs. Affectionately

Edward J. T

Don't tell anyone I am not to study a profession

⸺⟨∽⟩⸺

Saturday, 28 May 1853

Edward writes at last. He is to pursue business! Oh, shocking! Still, I am relieved to hear of his practical decision. I am relieved to hear from him at all! Such a vocation has served my father and our family well. Nevertheless, Edward announces this big news and then proceeds to write about mundane matters, as if nothing more needed to be said! Riding an unruly stallion like 'Major' is the least of my concerns.

I should be satisfied by his explanation for not writing, so am searching for every bit of patience I can summon, even considering 'existing circumstances.' I do not want to be an afterthought to him. Nor do I wish only to hear from him at his convenience. His well-being is certainly more important to me than that.

Although I am happy for what I hear, somehow, I am not a bit reassured of any matters of my heart. Surely he knows I have other suitors. Does this not matter to him? Does he expect I will wait with no word of his intention—lock myself in an attic until it is convenient for him to open the door? I do not mean to be unsympathetic about the demands on him, but he reverts to chatter of New York, 'spring shopping' and horseback riding, when more serious matters are at hand. I want to know what is in his heart. What does he long for when he wakes each morning? What is the business he is to do? What am I to expect?

Oh, dear. Perhaps this is what he anticipated from me when he asked that I not view him with a critic's eye. I must write at once and confess that a most critical Lizzie Andrews read his letter first and urged me to send a piece of her mind, but then came the Lizzie who thinks of Edward only with fondness and begged me to silence the critic and send a missive with the whole of my heart.

His silence and absence engulfed me with fear that the love of my life had taken a ship to another port—or a horse to another lady, as the case may be. If his heart is not with me, he should respectfully offer to return my letters. That would only be proper. Does he know nothing of the etiquette of courting?

Ah, but indeed, I only need a bit of hope or good reason from him, and I shall readily lock my door myself and await his knock. I would even send him the key, if he asks as much of me.

If I mail my letter on Monday, it will arrive in Methuen late Thursday. Edward can retrieve it at the post office Friday morning and if he responds by the Sabbath, I should hear some word by the week's end. For that I pray, and the rest will be as it may.

Friday, 3 June 1853

Father walked into the house this afternoon and gave me a very funny expression. He smiled in a way that made me think I had some coal ash smeared on my face or something untoward.

"How was your day, Father?" I asked. My question must have seemed just as curious to him as his expression was to me for he responded with, "Fine. Why do you ask?"

"You smiled, and I wondered if something might be amusing you."

"Nothing at all, my dear," he said. "In fact, I had some very serious business matters to discuss today."

Aunt Eliza entered the parlor and inquired of his day in a somewhat different manner. "Did your day pass as expected, Joseph?"

"Better than expected," he responded and said no more.

"Very well then, perhaps we might talk later," Aunt Eliza said, and sat silently on the chair next to Father.

Clearly, whatever happened today was not my concern. I excused myself and left the room, somewhat confused. Why had he looked at me so, and why were they so silent? Not certain if I really wished to end the conversation, I stopped in the hallway and pondered the situation.

My birthday has passed. Father usually confided in me about family matters. Aunt Eliza was not likely to inquire of Father regarding strictly business affairs. What was I missing? I stepped back toward the parlor, intending to query Father again, and overheard him conversing with Aunt Eliza. I stopped short of entering the room. Father has reprimanded me before for listening in on his conversations without announcing my presence. I could not pull away. Yet, I certainly could not step forward. Aunt Eliza murmured the name "Edward."

"Edward?" I popped into the room innocently, as if my appearance just that moment was a delightful coincidence.

"Lizzie!" Aunt Eliza said. "Were you eaves-dropping?"

"No!" I lied. "I only heard mention of Edward and came straight forward." Forgive me, my half-truth, I begged. Of all times, this was not a good time to fall out of favor with God.

"You've heard the saying 'curiosity killed the cat'?" she asked. She sighed and revealed, "Edward is coming for the Fourth of July. Now, it will not be a surprise. That is all."

"How delightful," I responded as if this was news to me, though I knew he was coming. It seemed, as Shakespeare might say, 'she doth protest too much!' That could not be all. "We will all look forward to his visit then, won't we?" I said lamely and smiled. There was something strange about the entire interaction. I look forward to hearing if Edward has any particular news.

⸙

Saturday, 4 June 1853

Edward should have received my letter yesterday. The morning was exceptionally quiet. Sea salt hung in the humid air, until the sun broke through and lifted the fog. When it did, I settled into a chair by the tea table in the parlor, and began to write in my diary.

I expected to pass the day like any other Saturday afternoon in spring, yet I was nearly overcome with the sense Edward must be writing me at that very moment. When next we meet, I must remember to ask if he was, in fact, writing me. The feeling sent a chill through me and made the hair stand on my flesh like goose skin.

I gathered a wrap from the hall-tree just as Laura announced, "Uncle John's buggy is approaching outside!" A horse clopping on the cobblestones slowed and stopped.

"John Fellows' carriage?" I asked.

"No, it is John Tenney's!" she responded enthusiastically.

I ran out the door to see Edward tethering his horse to the hitching post in front of the house. He would have had to depart his home quite early to arrive at this hour. The carriage appeared to be well packed. Clearly, this was not a hasty departure. He did not seem rushed in any manner. His expression revealed something weighing heavily on his mind.

As he began his approach up the short walk, I ran to the front door and called to him, "Edward! What is the matter?" He was only a few feet from me when he responded.

"The matter?" Edward climbed the steps to the porch, stopped in front of me and looked me in the eye, then glanced briefly at Laura, who was directly behind me in the doorway.

"I must seek your counsel, Lizzie. Have you the afternoon free to consult with me?" Edward glanced past me and I could almost feel Laura's eyes darting between Edward and me. I wanted to shoo her away like a pesky fly. I focused on Edward offering him a sober response. "Of course," I assured him.

"Laura, will you please excuse us?" Edward asked and beckoned me to move with him down the steps to the carriage and out of Laura's hearing range. She raised her eyebrows, and began to follow us but stopped outside and sat upon the step to watch the soundless show from afar. Edward paid her no mind as we proceeded toward his carriage. Bending closer, speaking only for my ear, he said, "Lizzie, I have come to respond to your letter in person, but we must be discreet. I will ask your father if you may accompany me on a visit to Methuen this afternoon, telling him that little Mamie is not well, and Aunt Laur needs your assistance for a couple of days. Of course, she needs my help, as well, since Uncle George is no longer around to help her."

"Mamie is not well?" I asked.

"That much is true. She has fallen ill and Dr. Holyoke has been called, but I have not heard specifically as to the nature of her illness."

"I do hope it is not serious," I said, a little too loud, in case big ears were nearby. "Certainly, we must help. Do ask Father if I may go with you and help you." Aunt Laur's home is not far from us in Salem. Edward's home was a full two hours by buggy from Salem; yet he made the trip back and forth with no complaints. He simply and calmly responded to whatever his widowed step-mother or Aunt Laur required. They both depended on him now and I was happy to help wherever I could.

Edward said, "I informed Mother my immediate attention was needed in Salem by mid-day on a matter that demanded a swift response."

"In Salem?" I was confused.

"I did not tell her I was needed at Aunt Laur's. I told her I needed to talk to you about a matter of concern with your family—something you mentioned in your letter. I promised her I would be back for church on Sunday, and upon my return would tell her what I had learned."

"What was in my letter that so concerned you for my family?" I asked, eagerly awaiting his response.

"Oh, Lizzie, it was what was in your heart when you *wrote* your letter…and what I felt in my own as I read it. That is the matter of concern for me in Salem. It was only after I departed that I formulated the excuse to tell your father." Edward paused and turned to me, "Lizzie, when I received your letter, I could not wait another moment to see you."

His sweet words fell upon my ears like a comforting lullaby and rang through my entire being. *Be still my heart!*

Laura's eyes focused on my back as we stood by the carriage. I did not want to wait another moment to depart with him. "You must speak with Father soon. Everyone is wondering what brings you here. We must go up to the house now, Edward."

Although my spirit was light, we walked with grave expressions up the front stairs to the porch. Laura managed to follow us up the steps into the house where the rest of the family gathered to see our guest and hear the news. Too often a surprise visit such as this was indicative of sad news—an untimely demise or other such tragedy. Occasionally, it was a welcome announcement of a birth, but those visits were anticipated and all that was left to say was 'mother and baby are faring well' or that one or both had not survived the battle to bring forth new life. Any time news was delivered in person all attention turned to the messenger and any other occupation stopped. Cookies, cakes, tea and sherry would magically appear, whether the news was cause for celebration or mourning. Edward expressed to Father an urgency to attend to Aunt Laur's needs to help care for little Frankie, and the situation with Mamie, one in which Father was somewhat familiar. It was soon settled that I should accompany him to Aunt Laur's. Edward told Father he would bring me to Methuen for church on Sunday and return me to Salem early Monday morning.

To my surprise, Father did not object! I bounded up the stairs and Aunt Eliza followed to help me ready myself for the trip and, as we returned, I heard Edward assure Father that the farmers were predicting a mild summer, but as long as I had my bonnet and parasol I should not be bothered by too much sun.

Aunt Eliza stood with Laura on the porch and bid us a good trip. Even Joe ventured out of the house to say good-bye.

We pulled away, maintaining a subdued affect. As we rode, the sun was high overhead. An offshore breeze wafted the scents of spring into the carriage. It was becoming warmer and Edward kept the horse at a slow gait. The Tenney's horse had been rather long in the pasture and the extended day trip could be demanding on him since the Senator had not left home for some time prior to his death. Edward, being committed to his father's bedside, certainly was not riding as much as he might have enjoyed.

Edward took a deep breath and let out a long sigh. I couldn't help but do the same, and we laughed with the kind of joy you see in school children who have not a care in the world. Edward drove the buggy to the edge of town. I could see the vast expanse of greening fields stretching into the distance. It seemed we had already passed Aunt Laur's.

"Whoa, boy." Edward steered the buggy to the side of the road.

"What is it?" I inquired. "Something's amiss?"

"It is you, dear Lizzie. You are a Miss," Edward said as he hopped down from the carriage. His voice faded as he passed in front of the horse mumbling, "but that will not always be the case."

"What nonsense are you uttering?" I asked. "Mustn't we be on our way?"

Edward was stopped at my side when he spoke. "We must not delay a moment longer." He grabbed a heavy wool blanket from behind my seat, then reached for my hand and helped me step down. His waistcoat gaped open exposing his linen shirt as he pulled me after him, the creases evidence of his long journey.

"Have you gone mad?" I asked. If he had, I was certain to join him for I could not stop myself from following his lead, my skirts billowing behind me and my feet flying beneath the hems. Edward had not a touch of his previously somber mood. He smiled as if he knew a secret. His mood was utterly contagious. I began to giggle, but caught myself, remembering Aunt Laur awaited our arrival. This was no time to dillydally. We were being naughty, but what misfortune could possibly befall us if this detour delayed our arrival? We would be only slightly later. Edward moved quickly and had I not been at the end of his arm, I surely would not have kept stride.

Finally, he let go of me and took the blanket he had tucked under his arm shaking it loosely onto the grassy field.

"Please sit, Lizzie. I have a confession to make."

What now? I thought, and sat as best I could, folding my limbs beneath me, my dress tucked around and under them. I waited for him to speak. He stood above me and let his eyes drop as if he were surveying the awkward position in which I perched. Then, he looked me directly in the eye.

In a deep, soft voice he began, "How I have missed feasting my eyes on your beauty. You are a vision of loveliness, like no other."

He seemed to gather his thoughts and I braced myself for his confession, my mind racing. Had he given himself to another woman out of desperation? Was this admiration stemming from remorse, or was it due to our prolonged separation? Margie had surely been at his side recently and their late evening rides beneath a rising moon must have put her in a romantic mood. I had not seen her, nor heard a word of news about her one way or the other. Surely, my letter had convinced him that absence does indeed make one's heart grow fonder. I assumed he understood the reference was to my heart, not hers! Now, I regretted having made the suggestion. Perhaps his heart had grown fonder, too—but not for me.

"Lizzie, you are the most beautiful woman I have ever seen." He paused.

"That is an unusual confession, but I am listening. Go on," I urged him to continue, expecting he would break my heart and get on with his news, but he laughed.

"You want more? You are insatiable, my dear Lizzie!" He dropped to his knees, laughing so hard he tipped onto his side. Then, he rolled on his back laughing. His face filled with an expression of supreme joy.

"Edward! You are completely cruel to laugh so. Now, stop." I did not understand this man.

He sat up. "You want me to say more about your beauty? Is it not enough that I confess you are the loveliest lady I have ever set my eyes upon?"

"*That* is your confession?" I was flushed with embarrassment and utterly confused. I raised my voice now to be heard over this boisterous guffaw. "I am braced to hear you confess that you have given your heart to another!"

"My word!" he stopped short and his look was one of shock. "How could I?" He shifted himself so he sat and leaned against my side, reaching his arm around my shoulders. He held me, and spoke softly into my ear. "Lizzie. Lizzie. I think of *nothing but you* day in and day out. There is no other that has come into my heart, my dear, dear Lizzie. None other ever will. Everything I do is for you." He radiated warmth and was so close I could feel his breath. He seemed to breathe mine in, his face was so near to me. "My sweet, sweet Lizzie," he continued. "I am forever yours, my darling Lizzie." He leaned over and kissed me, first lightly on the cheek and then on the side of my mouth.

I turned to look at him. He moved his hands to my face and pulled me toward him, my lips landing directly on his so I could not easily move away. His lips were sweet and soft; his breath was sweet and warm. I did not want to move away, of course, but had it been a simple maneuver I would have certainly done the proper thing and righted myself immediately. He wrapped his arms around my waist and I fell like Newton's apple, surrendering, perhaps too readily as we rolled together across the blanket. Soon I was on my back and he was above me, looking so lovingly into my face. My whole body tingled. I did not care that some lone farmer might pass and see me swooning in his arms. An apple must fall when the tree is shaken. Sir Isaac proved as much. Gravity was something more than I could control. Edward kissed and held me for a very long time. Our breathing fell into one rhythm.

"I love you, Lizzie," Edward said, and then he pulled away. I rolled on my side, suddenly self-conscious, and pushed myself up until I was sitting.

Edward placed one foot on the ground, but instead of rising to his feet, he stayed on one knee, leaned toward me and began, "I have had much time to pray and contemplate about what I should pursue in my life. As I nursed my father and tended to his business at his bedside, I searched my heart and found nothing more important to me than you. I want to live my life with you and for you. I want to offer you something no other man can. I want to have a family… with you as my wife and the mother of my children."

I began to respond, but he touched his fingers to my mouth.

"Let me continue. I know we are too young to begin such a serious courtship, but I must know if this is wild foolishness on my part or if this could be your dream as well." He paused, still looking directly into my eyes. I felt a rush of warmth come over me, a sensation of peacefulness. Before I could say a word, he continued.

"Lizzie, will you marry me? Will you be my wife? Will you spend the rest of your life with me…spend the rest of our lives together?"

I answered promptly in my mind, but the words did not leave my lips. That brief moment was timeless. Inside, I was crying with joy at the top of my voice but, as in a dream, what came through was merely a breathy whisper struggling to find a voice.

"Yes," I finally emitted as my mind raced. There is no other. There would never be another for me. I was to be his. It was what I had longed for. I did not know if I should laugh for joy or cry out of relief.

"Are you sure?" Edward asked, not understanding how all that was in my heart had struggled to make its way to my throat.

"Oh, yes!" I found my voice. "I love you, too. I have always loved you, and I want nothing more than to make you happy…as your wife."

Now it was my turn to confess. "Edward, I feared I had lost you, that your heart had been turned away from me. So great was my fear, that I became mired in the depth of my own sorrow—a sadness I hoped you would never know. It was your absence that helped me see the emptiness of my life without you. I love you, my darling. I will love you forever."

"Oh, Lizzie, I cannot tell you how I have longed to hear such words from your lips—perfect words from your most perfect mouth." He sat on the blanket again and continued. "I know you have been in the company of Whittemore. When I received your last letter I feared the worst. My neglected darling had found another to care for her, one who might take better care of her, too. I could only blame myself if you were to refuse my company for another who was more attentive—one who could escort you dancing and treat you to the fine pleasures you desire. But no one could love you more than I. It simply is not possible. My love for you is immense."

I smoothed the silk on my skirt, stroking the ribbons back in place, but my eyes remained fixed on the most gentle, clever and handsome man I had ever known.

"I will gladly forsake the company of any other, now that we are betrothed," I assured him. I wanted nothing more than to reveal my love for him. "Should you leave, your absence will only allow me to more thoroughly prepare to become your wife, but I shall begin now to devote my own self only to you. I do not mind waiting, as I know we must, to reveal our engagement. Now that I know what is to be, my patience will be … endless."

"You have made me so completely happy, my dear." Edward gave me a soft, gentle kiss on the lips. "But there is one more thing I must ask."

"Yes?" I asked with slight trepidation. What more could he ask of me? I wondered, fearing the worst. Certainly he would not expect …

Edward laughed. "Lizzie, my dear, dear girl. You look terrified. I simply want to ask if, in keeping our engagement private, you might want to address me by a pet name. 'Edward' is what everyone calls me. What we have is special, deserving of a name that is special. I would welcome any desire you might have to call me something other."

Feeling great relief that this was all he asked of me at this time, I responded, "Oh no, I could never call you 'something other.'" I laughed. "'Something other' is so utterly impersonal!" I continued. "I would need to find a truly special name for you. Let me think. It must be manly and distinguished, like you. I could never call you 'baby.' It must be strong and powerful. I could never call you 'darling.' It must be ever so sophisticated. I could never call you 'honey.' Hmmm. Why, I think I shall simply call you my Ned. May I call you Ned? No one else does. It could be ours alone."

"Of course, you may," he leaned toward me and placed a kiss of approval on my very lips. "I will be your Ned, my dear darling, my pet."

"Then, by what pet name shall you call me?"

He paused, and said, "It must be a name that shows my devotion, a name that reassures you I will take care of you, I will be faithful and you shall never want for anything…a name that shows how I cherish and adore you." He paused again as he thought. "Lizzie, each time you greet me you radiate love and acceptance; and when it is time for me to depart from your precious company, I am loathe to go. I dare say you are my true pet—someone who I trust will be by my side as my companion for life and remain true and faithful to me as I will be to you. I will call you 'my pet.'" He leaned toward me and held my face in his warm hands to plant a row of kisses along my cheeks and lips.

We lingered for some time, speaking of things neither of us had ever revealed to a living soul. The sun had passed across the field and shadows began to grow from nearby trees.

"Edward, is not Aunt Laur expecting us?"

"I suppose I have another confession for you. I failed to tell the entire truth to your family. It is true that Mamie has fallen ill, but not too seriously. It is true that Aunt Laur needs us, but not that she asked us to come. I could think of no other way to steal you from your home without raising suspicion."

"Edward! You told my father a fib? Is this what I am to expect of you in the future? I must grow very clever to keep your half-truths from deceiving me!" Edward laughed at my scolding, for nothing could spoil our delicious afternoon.

"You know I must make an appearance at Aunt Laur's or I will raise a *great deal* of suspicion upon my return home." I accepted this as my role to ensure that we were respectable, and *beyond* reproach.

"Why, of course, we will go to Aunt Laur's, and we will be welcomed. Our assistance will be helpful. My plan was in the best interests of all concerned, my dear Lizzie. You can rest assured, my intentions are pure. In fact, your father has already given me his consent."

Relationship Chart

Edward and Lizzie are 3rd cousins once removed

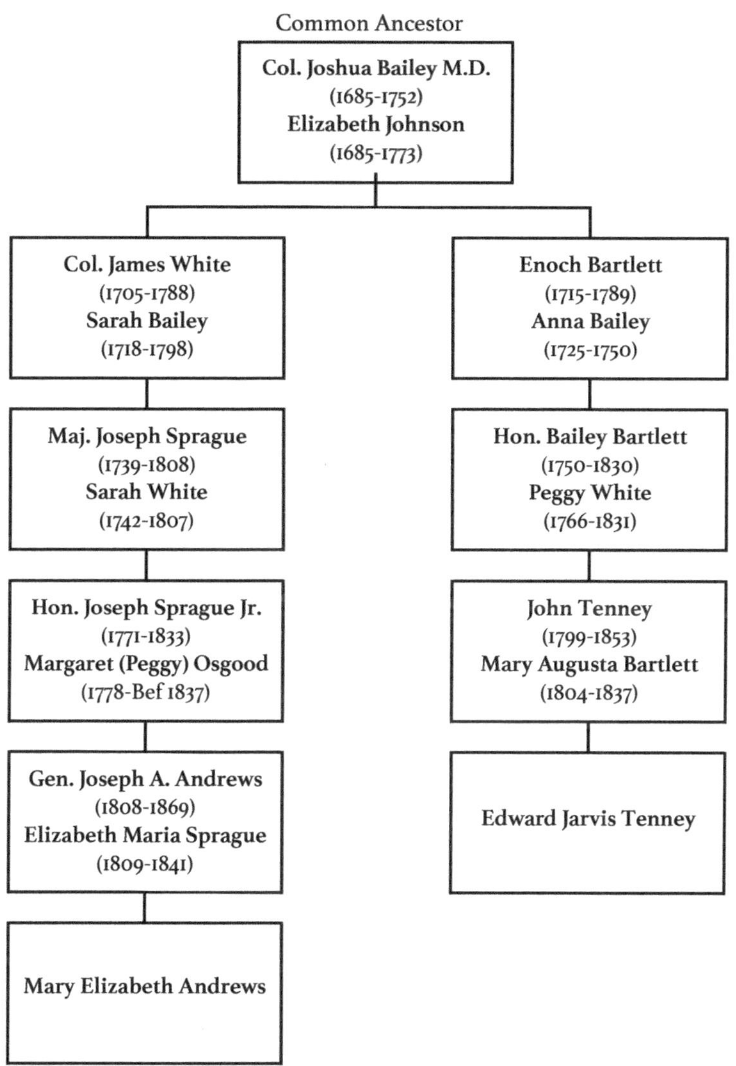

Relationship Chart

"He has?" I stopped my futile efforts to move toward a timely departure.

"I spoke with him yesterday in his office. You can be sure I have a solid plan for our lives together. I now know the right thing to do and will not do wrong by you." Edward stood and helped me to my feet.

"Father knows? What does he know?"

"He knows everything. Well, almost everything," Edward laughed. "He gave me his permission to ask for your hand, and he gave us his blessing, Lizzie. He did not do so quickly, however."

"Oh, my!"

"Lizzie, he asked me if I knew the true nature of our cousinly relationship."

"Absurd! He knows Augusta is my mother's sister."

"He knows more than that, my dear, dear cousin. He knows more than we do! You are my cousin, by blood."

"Oh, no! Then, how can we marry?"

"But, joy of all joys, your Father says it is acceptable for us to marry, since we are not first cousins! We are third cousins."

"We are? How can that be?"

"Your Father explained. Let me recall." He seemed to be searching the heavens for the words. Then spoke slowly, counting the generations on his fingers, "Your mother's father's grandmother was a sister to my mother's grandmother."

"Oh my!"

"Lizzie, my darling love, do not fret. We are meant to be together. We have your father's blessing. We can have everything we could ever dream of. Of course, we need to work for it, but I am prepared to do that, now more than ever, for I have you to work for, and our future together. Your father also approved of my plans for my new enterprise."

"Edward, what does he know? Have you made solid plans?"

"So, you think I should tell *you* as well?"

"Well, yes, *I do*, you rascal," I scolded. "What did you tell my Father?

"I like the way you say 'I do,' Lizzie." Edward seemed to enjoy keeping me in suspense.

"Well! Is this a sign of what is to be with you? Pray tell."

"Fine. Fine. No more teasing. I will tell you happily." He began, "All these days and weeks I have been traveling to Boston and New York have not been in vain. I have before me a most promising position working as a clerk on a new steamer ship that is journeying to Valparaiso, Chile. Lizzie, do you know where that is?"

"I know where Chile is, but not Valparaiso."

"It is in the middle of Chile and is the busiest seaport in that country—the busiest port in the southern half of South America, maybe the busiest port along South America's entire west coast! Ships traveling to San Francisco pass through Valparaiso, and nearly all enter its harbor for a short stay to deliver goods. Then they export copper, other minerals, metals and foodstuffs like fish and agriculture. Lizzie, they also have fine textiles. Your father has imported some textiles from Chile and we spoke of the opportunities I might find."

"Oh, Edward, you must not stay and seek opportunities away from me!"

"Heavens no! That is not my intent. I am only thinking of how I can support you, Lizzie. And of course, now that my father has died, I must provide for my mother and my sisters until each is married. As a merchant, I can do this.

"As a merchant? But you must have wealth to establish yourself as a merchant, Edward!"

"I do not mean immediately, but someday I will be able to export goods from New England to South America and on to San Francisco, or from Chile back to New York or even Europe. I have seen how this is done, Lizzie. I have met with men who do this. They showed me how they hire sailors to do the work. There is so much promise, Lizzie. The sailors call Valparaiso 'Little San Francisco.' Of course, they say it in Spanish, un poco San Francisco."

"You will need to speak Spanish?"

"Yes, of course. I have studied some Spanish, so I am certain to pick it up well enough once I am there. That is the least of the necessary preparations, my darling. The sailing will be the most difficult. One must sail to nearly the bottom of the world and circumnavigate South America. It can be very dangerous to cross through the Straights of Magellan due to unpredictable winds and currents. The channel is very narrow. It takes great skill. Valparaiso is such a busy port that Chile is only recently reclaiming control from Spain and England. A little more than a decade ago the Pacific Steam Navigation Company used its first steam ships for commerce in this region. Uncle Edwin is a partner in that company."

"Edward, but what will *you* do? You are not yet a wealthy merchant and certainly not a sailor! What will you do with a Harvard education? More importantly, how will you be safe?"

"Initially, I will work at a desk as a clerk, Lizzie. I have been studying all the laws and training in practices one must follow to manage the accounts of the merchants and the ship owners. They have shown me how to keep the record books. That is my charge. I will write the ledgers to show which goods came on board and how much each is worth. I will document which sailors are retained for the journey and how great a payment to provide them when we are at port. Uncle Edwin says this experience will provide me a solid foundation for managing a business of my own someday, perhaps even owning a business like your father does.

"Lizzie, someday I may build my own ship. I will be paid handsomely and can provide support to you and to Mother and my sisters and little brother. Most importantly, I will be able to support our children. Should your own father or brother be unable to support your sister until she marries, I may be in a position to help. I am being trained by clever and successful men, like Uncle Edwin. After a few years, I will not need to voyage on the ships myself. I will provide opportunities to younger men to learn. I will stay in port in Salem with you and our children. This is my opportunity to secure a substantial salary, so I may buy you a fine home right here."

I looked at him and could see the excitement in his eyes. He was full of hope and I wanted to feel that too. I did feel it, but I felt cautious, and I think he could see that. I had no words to adequately express my fear, excitement, hope and concern. He continued to talk.

"Lizzie, I will be gone only three years at most."

"Three years is so long, Edward."

"It is not certain if I will go on to San Francisco or remain in Valparaiso while the *San Francisco* completes its journey. My orders will await me there from Uncle Edwin's associates. If there is opportunity for me to be of more use to the business by staying in port for a while, I will do that.

"How long will you be at sea?"

"The journey to Valparaiso takes just over two months—70 days at best. If I continue to San Francisco it is another 16 days."

"…and back again."

"Yes, in all I will travel on board for only two months, but I will be all the time working, even in port. Oh, Lizzie, it is not an easy decision. I do hope you will support me as your father has. He had many questions for me about my intent. Nearly as many as you! I had to assure him that we had done nothing wrong and that I would not compromise you in any way. He said he trusts me, Lizzie. As hard as it might be for me to resist rushing, I will remain worthy of his trust."

"And I will remain true to you, my dear, silly Ned. I will remain faithful only to you and will cherish each day I wait for you."

"I told your father that should I be so lucky as to have you for my fiancé I thought it best that we keep our engagement a secret until I return. I will be worthy of you one day, Lizzie, but I must work hard first. You have made me the happiest man alive and I promise you will not regret that."

We returned to the carriage at half the pace that led us away from the carriage just hours earlier. No time seemed to pass before we were upon Aunt Laur's house. Edward helped me from the carriage with such kindness I could not help but think how utterly spectacular my life will be as his wife.

✽ *Valparaiso, Chile, South America*

My musings continued at a furious pace as we entered the house. Her small house in Salem was perfectly fit for her small family. Now, with Uncle George gone, the house was too much for her to care for alone. Her time and attention was with her children. With two little ones, she was little able to continue her millinery work, so while her home was a convenient location for her customers, she was talking about moving to live with other family.

As she greeted us, little Frankie hid behind her, standing on wobbly legs, clinging to her skirts. Aunt Laur hurried us in and closed the door behind us, just as the kettle began to whistle. Mamie was curled up in the corner of the davenport.

"Mama," she whimpered. Aunt Laur headed toward Mamie, with Frankie in tow.

"Edward, would you be so kind as to fetch the kettle for tea?"

"Of course." Edward eagerly complied. He looked inquisitively at me. He must have known I was about to offer to help, until Aunt Laur asked a favor of me.

"Please, Lizzie, see to Frankie, will you?" she asked, not waiting for a response. "I am so glad you have just now arrived, as I seem to need just one more hand at all times." She did not need a verbal reply from me. I drifted toward little Frankie and bent down to lift the frail boy into my arms. He was such a tiny thing; his cheeks so pink and soft. He looked to me younger than sixteen months. He reached his arms around my neck and curled his little body into mine. Aunt Laur was happy to let me rock him to sleep. I was so happy to hold him and comfort him.

Aunt Laur stroked Mamie's forehead. With both children at ease and the kettle calm, she quickly engaged in conversation with Edward.

"When is class-day, Edward? What are your plans thereafter? Will you stay in Methuen?"

He filled her in, speaking in hushed tones. There was a comfortable air about her little home. I imagined the adult conversation was a refreshing change from her mothering and nursing duties, and I was delighted to assist, though I added little to the conversation, for news of my engagement was a secret. The only thing on my mind was my fiancé and the breathing of the sweet little child in my lap.

Gazing first at little Frankie, Edward glanced at me, "You look as if you would be a wonderful mother, Lizzie," he said. His comment seemed abrupt and much too personal a remark coming from a cousin. Aunt Laur's attention had turned back to Mamie and I am not sure she even heard.

Having no idea what an appropriate response might be to Edward, I spoke to Aunt Laur, "He is such a sweet boy, is he not?"

"He is very sweet, indeed, especially when he is sleeping. He struggles so when he is awake. He seems to have such a frail constitution. I worry," Aunt Laur disclosed.

As soon as I laid him down next to Mamie, he woke and began to fuss with the tiniest of cries, more like a soft whimper. Aunt Laur picked him up right away, and held him close to her heart. They seemed to comfort each other. He was flushed, and his warm little face became imprinted with the pattern of lace from her bodice, as if her dress were ironed into his soft fleshy cheek.

Once both children were sound asleep, Edward helped Aunt Laur take them to her bed. She showed me where I could sleep in Mamie's room and provided Edward a wool blanket and feather pillow to sleep on the davenport. She bid us each a good night. The children seemed to sleep through the night.

We helped Aunt Laur in the morning with breakfast. With the children fed, cleaned and dressed, and breakfast dishes put away, I started a pot of soup simmering on the stove for dinner and we departed for Edward's home.

We arrived in time to transport the Tenney family to the final Sunday service of the day at the Methuen Congregational Church. He dropped me off first with Mary, Margie and Johnnie, and returned home for Lottie, Aunt Augusta and baby Augusta. Once at church, we joined our friend Margie Phillips for her father's sermon.

Methuen Congregational Church service

As soon as the service ended, we brought Aunt Augusta and the children home and took our time traveling around the countryside, Edward sharing all the places he roamed as a child, all the places his father helped develop. By the time we arrived back at his home Sunday night, all the lights were extinguished and not a soul was awake to welcome us.

We sat for a short time to talk by candlelight and I shared with Edward my gratitude for his devotion to his … to our … family, and to me.

Edward helped me find my way to Liz's empty room remarking, "I am tempted to bring you across this narrow hall to my own room, but I think the sermon on resisting temptation was for my benefit and I must do right by you."

"Pardon me?" I pretended I had not heard him. He kissed me quietly as he turned me to Liz's bed. I slipped off my outer dresses, unlaced my shoes and fell quickly to slumber in my cousin Liz's chambers.

The next morning, we woke with the sun to begin our carriage ride right back to Salem.

My sorrow in leaving him was immense. I felt as if my own heart was being pulled from my breast and I worried how I might feel when my Edward departs for Valparaiso.

<hr>

Saturday, 11 June 1853

Edward came back to Salem today. He arrived in time for dinner and joined us for vegetable barley soup and sandwiches on freshly baked bread with meats, cheeses, cucumbers and tomatoes. We spent the afternoon together in the garden helping Aunt Eliza. She has several large trays of vegetable starts that were ready to be planted. She was delighted to have Edward's help with some of the hoeing and hauling. Aunt Eliza asked Joe to help mix fertilizer into the soil but he was less inclined to get his hands dirty than either Edward or I. The sun was bright but not too hot. We were able to chat freely with each other and Aunt Eliza. All of this made for a very pleasant, relaxing afternoon. We helped Aunt Eliza select an assortment of annual flower starts she could bring to Grandmother for her planter garden.

After supper, Aunt Eliza took the plants to Grandmother's and Edward and I enjoyed a long evening together reading out loud in the parlor. Although Edward is staying the night with Joe, Joe did not have any interest in reading with us, so he retreated to his room early. Father stayed nearby reading in his office. Laura was upstairs with her nose in *Godey's*.

"At least she reads!" I offered. We were both relieved that others were content to allow us some privacy; however, it was not all that private with Father so nearby.

Aunt Augusta wants Edward back in Methuen in the morning to drive her to Salem so she can check on Aunt Laur. Surely the two sisters are glad to spend time together after these most difficult losses for each of them. Aunt Laur knew all too recently the despair her younger sister Augusta must still be experiencing after her husband died.

Edward thinks Aunt Laur will move to Methuen with her children and live with his family. Such a move would make Edward the man of the house for both these widows and their eight children, who range in age from infant to 18—if you include his sister Liz, who is the same age as me. Edward is already assuming responsibilities for both families, so having them all in one place might be a relief.

Edward has told me I must not awkwardly cancel any engagement I have made to accompany Whittemore so as not to raise suspicion, but certainly I will refrain from any further engagements with anyone other than Edward.

Lizzie waters Aunt Eliza's garden

I agreed to attend class-day at Harvard, and am to join him there, two weeks from today. Soon after, he is to depart by ship, perhaps for some time and to places far from me, but I will remain steadfast. We talked much of patience and holding each other's faith; even when demands pull us from each other's presence. Our hearts and our minds will not stray. I am so utterly happy.

⁕

Friday, 17 June 1853

Could love be the cause of my sudden idleness? While others are busying about in preparation for summer solstice events, I am content to sit with Grandmother in the garden daydreaming. She thinks I concentrate on my fancywork, but my focus is on Edward—of one who is more kind and generous than any who has walked the earth. His goodness inside is only matched by his handsomeness outside.

I suppose it is just as well I cannot see Edward today, for on the first day of summer I will be escorted by someone other than the one I love. I must not let on. I have had too few idle moments lately and cherish the contentment I feel today. I must be patient. Our time will come and when it does, we will have many happy years and, by the grace of God, many healthy children. That is the dream I hold in my heart. The heartache of my imprudence is gone—pierced from my breast by Cupid's arrow. It has shot through me and I have surrendered to love.

II. Secretly Bethrothed

In Edward and Lizzie's social circles in 1850s Salem, there was a proper time and place for a public announcement of an engagement. Until that time, keeping an engagement a secret was appropriate and challenging. As young gentlemen and ladies approached marrying age, speculations were often made and had to be discredited or corroborated.

M. Lizzie Andrews.
(of all the fair, the fairest.)

CHAPTER 7

I Never Knew Joy Before

Miss Lizzie Andrews
Care of Gen. J. Andrews
Salem,
Mass.

Methuen, [Friday] June 17th, 1853

My dear Lizzie –

I have been in Cambridge today to inquire about class-day etc. etc. and to see what time you had better leave Salem. Ladies with tickets are admitted to the Chapel at 11 A.M. so you will be in season if you leave Salem in the 9 o'clock train.

I will meet you in Boston when the cars arrive and accompany you to Cambridge. If it would not trouble you too much, I would like to have you invite in my name Katy Downing, Caddie Roberts, Sarah Stearns, Lucy and Mary Osgood or whoever of them may be at home. Please explain why I did not ask them myself, i.e. because I was undecided about going, and make them all come if you can. I should also be pleased to see Laura and Joe if they will come. If you wish to ask any one else whom I have forgotten of course I shall be delighted to have you do so. I expect no one else but Emily Oliver and I have prepared for an indefinite number under 100. Tell Willie Carlton to come if you meet him. I shall send a note to JW. "The more the merrier," so if you think of any one I can or should like to see, persuade them to come. I shall expect a letter from you before Friday and if you can, conveniently, write by Monday or Tuesday, I shall know whom to look for.

Since I left Salem I have felt as happy and good as possible. I took the best possible care of Mamie Allen all the way up while Frank cried the whole time, and when I reached home I felt like kissing every one in the whole house. I was almost tipsy with delight. And just think, Lizzie, what I have gained; no more doubt; no more jealousy nor anxiety. I am now sure of being loved as well as I can love and hurrah! Excuse me, dearest, but I never knew joy before and I can't control myself. I have thought of 10,000 things I ought to have said, since I left you. To remind me of one very important thing please ask me when we meet, if I know "Mr. Whipple." Now don't try to guess what I mean, for you can't possibly imagine it. If my letters are silly now, forgive me, but I shan't try to reform at present.

I have been looking over some parts of my journal, and reading pages which I should delight to show you, though I could not have done so a week ago. We must try and see as much of each other as possible while I am here, for God only knows, when we may meet again. Of one thing I am fully determined; that your brother Joe shall not stay at home while I am gone if I can help it. If nothing else will do I will do my best to persuade him to go away with me. For the thought of leaving one dearer than all the world in the hands of such a brother(!) is not to be entertained.

How much easier I should feel if you had such a home as I could choose for you, and how great a change from your present home. But it does no good to harp on what can not be helped, and I pray you may be spared all suffering. I know you have tried to do your best and I think you deserve great praise for coming through such a trial safely.

Did you ever find it so hard to keep a secret before? I have wanted to tell every one what a prize I have gained in hopes that they will feel as much elated as I am. Still I have not changed my mind in regard to our engagement being private, and I still think it would be unwise to announce it to the world.

I saw Whittemore in Cambridge today: he asked if I had been in Salem lately, if I had seen "the folks." I answered yes to both questions and he said no more on that subject. You need have no fears about meeting him next Friday, for that can be very easily arranged without trouble. I only wish that I dared to dance; for then you need no more than speak with him. If JW comes up there will not be the least difficulty, but I do not expect to see him.

Emily Oliver's friend Mr. Briggs, was dreadfully "snubbed" (excuse that word) in the cars this morning. I will tell you about it on class-day if I don't forget it.

Be sure and come on Friday, whether it rains or not; for if it should be unpleasant I shall still have as good an opportunity to tell you many things you must know. What a difference in our feelings has a few moments made; now I feel as free and open with you as with myself. I could conceal nothing from you, and yet at the same time I have not the least fear of your ever being displeased at what I may say or do. I wish I could be with you all the time till I would go to work and then I should go ahead with much more earnestness than before, conscious that I was labouring for your sake.

I don't believe you will ask me to return your letters now, shall you? Because if you do, why then—you can't have them. I am afraid your father will think I am writing you too soon after leaving Salem, but you can tell him about invitations for class-day etc. Please tell me who will come when you write. Will you please send me one of your cards in your letters if the size is just

what you want? I will try and make some more for you a little
better than the last.

After all my care I left Emily Oliver's basket in Salem. But
she told me today she had not needed it, as it was too delicate
for carrying flowers. If you will take care of that I will take it
some time. I hope you may receive this by Saturday night
so that I may hear from you very soon. I shall probably go to
Cambridge on Thursday and stay till Saturday. Tell your father
that you may have to stay over Friday night, for if I can find a
good excuse I shall keep you till Saturday. Good night—

Edward

Monday, 20 June 1853

I read Edward's letter and began planning how I might invite all
who he requested be present at his commencement. They are nearly
all girls, so that should not be a problem for me. However, Edward
requests Willie Carlton attend. I cannot think of dear Willie without
recalling the grief he and his family endured when his older brother,
Edwin Bartlett Carlton, was lost at sea just two years ago. Perhaps Joe
will assist me. Perhaps not, I thought again.

I am very pleased to be the one he asked to invite Katy Downing,
as that will show her how very close I am with my cousin. Surely Katy
would happily extend the invitation to Caddie Roberts. I can easily
walk by Sarah's house on Essex and Dean and deliver an invitation
this week-end. I wonder why Edward said JW is not expected to come.
Perhaps Sarah knows. Father may be willing to extend the invitation
to Aunt Mary and Cousin Lucy when he goes to town. I hope to see
Emily Oliver at the train station next week so will encourage her to
invite her friend Mr. Briggs as she seems quite fond of him and we
certainly have a lot of ladies and a shortage of escorts. I cannot count
on my own brother to be reliable in that manner.

Friday, 24 June 1853

Tomorrow is Edward's class-day at Harvard. I will be up at the crack of dawn to get ready for the 9:00 a.m. train to Cambridge. Willie Carlton, Sarah Stearns, Katy Downing, Lucy and Mary Osgood plan to meet me at the Salem station so we may ride together in the cars. Edward is meeting us at the station. Emily Oliver will be coming by train from Lawrence. I am utterly excited!

This is not the first class-day I have attended, as Edward has invited me before. It is the most important, however, since he is graduating. I missed the first class-day in 1850. I later heard so much about Governor Edward Everett's oration I regretted that I had not been there. Edward Everett was known to draw a massive crowd anywhere he was to speak. I was overwhelmed by the thought of the crowds pushing me into the hall only to stand in the heat. I was sure I would not be able to see the orator, nor hear him, due to the din of so many people. I was certain I would faint. I had never been alone with so many strangers before. So, I fled back to Salem. The next year, Edward was in Warren, so I had no invitation to class-day. Last year, I was determined to stay and had a glorious time. I sat with Edward and his chum Wilson.

Each year, the ladies are dressed in their very best, so this year I have a new dress Edward has not yet seen. It is a walking dress of lemon-colored silk with raised satin stripes and blue trimmings and decoration. The skirt has four flounces. The stomacher is covered with blue ribbon knots, which also trim the square neckline and open, demi-long sleeves. I have a simple headdress with the same ribbon knots patterned to form rosettes. The undersleeves are ivory lace. My shawl is of the same lace with the blue ribbon knots as trim. I hope he likes the dress on me.

Celebrating Edward's class-day

Monday, 4 July 1853

Oh, it is a glorious day. The air in Salem is crisp and the sky is bright. I do not see how this day can seem so much prettier than any other; surely it is not an illusion. Yes, it is a celebratory day of our Independence, and there is much ado as people ready for the grand festivities tonight. I have had the pleasure of Edward hosting me on class-day in Cambridge, which was everything I had hoped it would be with so many to congratulate him. He is nearly famous, or infamous, on campus as a result of his expulsion. To top it off, he thought my dress to be the finest he had ever seen. Now, I am to host him for Independence Day festivities and I expect his arrival in Salem any moment.

Anticipation fills me like a breeze of fresh air. Is this not the same air I breathed last week? I am certain it settles differently in me now. Just two months ago, my heart felt cold and resigned and I complained to Edward in my hasty missive. He said my letter was the first he had seen of my true passion. Imagine that! Instead of being frightened away,

Edward came immediately so as not to lose me.

Edward arrived much like he had a month ago, but this time he quieted his horse and cautiously proceeded around the house to the garden. We embraced in the garden, hidden by the fullness of the magnolia tree out of sight of any windows. We were deliciously reckless with our affections. I was hardly behaving like a lady when Laura saw me accept a prolonged kiss from Edward. We cannot be solely to blame for our display, however, for Laura has a manner about her that allows her to be nearly invisible. We did not even hear the rustle of her skirt to alert us to her approach until she was well upon us. Then, her presence could not be denied or ignored. She appeared suddenly behind me, sneaking along the garden path like a field rat. She spoke loudly with shock and disdain in her voice, saying only one word, "Edward!"

He pulled his face from mine and stepped away abruptly. Every bit of color fell from his face, but his recovery was quick. He put on a charming smile and greeted Laura with as much kindness as if she had asked for directions to church. I stepped aside, wishing I could *absquatulate* without being seen, or somehow disappear through the house's brickwork, as Laura seemed to have done.

"Hello, Laura, so nice to see you." Edward's calm voice was in sharp contrast to the torture that wretched my own.

"Edward is going to Valparaiso, or perhaps San Francisco!" I spoke, as if to excuse my behavior, my face burning with a sour mix of anger and shame. Only then did I realize what I had revealed to her—Edward's private plans, which he had trusted me to safeguard.

"Oh, that I could go, too!" Laura surprised us both. She looked longingly at Edward, our stunned faces momentarily frozen like thespian masks.

"Laura, you are not yet 15! How could you even think such a thing?" I scolded her vehemently, partly to divert her attention from what she had witnessed.

Edward continued with calm persuasion. "Laura, you must not say a thing about it, for it is too soon to announce my plans. My travel is months away and my plans are yet uncertain." Edward convinced her. "So not a word now. About anything. Can I count on you?"

"I suppose." She twirled on one foot, her skirts brushing his pant leg as she swept away, a gaggle of long blond ringlets bouncing behind her head as she marched.

We stood stunned and silent for several minutes, not even touching each other. I saw a tear in Edward's eye and dabbed it with my handkerchief.

"I'm so sorry, Lizzie. I should not have taken such liberties with you. I wanted so much to kiss you like that at class-day but we had not one moment alone. It is so hard for me to restrain myself when I am near you. You are so beautiful."

I reached up and put my arms around his neck and pulled him to my heart, "Let us not be sorry for anything," I said. "I love you, my sweet, sweet Ned."

This 4th of July, each member of my family went a separate way. Rather than celebrate together, Aunt Dolly and Father walked to the park. Uncle Daniel stayed home with Grandmother. Joe visited JW. Laura went about with several girlfriends. The help was on holiday, so Aunt Eliza stayed home and tended to tasks.

By evening, we were free to promenade at the square, every bit of decorum being necessary. The darkness in between fireworks displays tempted us to forget we were not alone. More than once our intimate conversations were interrupted by an acquaintance or a passerby.

"Oh, Edward. Can we just escape and go far from here?"

Edward looked around and beckoned toward a spot under a tree. "Would that suit you more comfortably?" He asked.

"I do not mean this moment, silly. I mean forever after," I clarified. I wished to flee from the intrusions of my sister and the outbursts from my brother. I told Edward things about my brother that I had never shared with anyone, not even in my letters, for they revealed such matters as were not often discussed even within families. I confessed that I wanted to go with him to some completely new world—I did not care where. Perhaps I could stow-away on a ship to Valparaiso. My fanciful vision hit hard against Edward's responsible agenda. I knew my vision was but a dream. I just wanted my life to be another way, and did not hesitate to express myself, though I felt a bit like a spoiled child when I did.

We walked back to the house in the dark with only the slightest crescent moon and street lamps to light our way. The rest of our family seemed to go about other business that night, and appeared to be fine leaving us to sit alone in the garden on the wicker love seat where we talked late into the night about such matters as only two entrusted to each other might reveal.

"I must be back in Boston early tomorrow morning," Edward finally admitted. "I really must be off to bed and let Joe see that I arrive to share his room. No sense raising more suspicion. It is best if I leave at daybreak."

I caught him in the morning as he tried to leave quietly and surely shocked him by appearing in nothing more than my nightgown covered by my morning cloak to bid him good-bye. No one else in the household was awake, but Edward was not the only one to be out and about so early. A carriage passed by in full view of me waving from the front porch. Oh, scandal! There was nothing to do but slip inside as quickly as I could. With that, Edward was on his way.

***

Tuesday, 5 July 1853

San Francisco! That is where I wanted to go. I could not remove the thought from my mind of traveling to San Francisco. Oh, absurd. What am I thinking? Such a journey is much too difficult for me I am certain. There are only two ways to reach San Francisco, and neither traversing overland through Indian Territory, nor travel by unruly seas, was for me. Should I manage to survive such a trip, how could I manage to live? We have not money sufficient for servants and I am in no way well-seasoned enough to survive as a pioneer woman. Edward and I would both surely wither away to nothing without the support of family. Heavens! We would have to live on sponge cake and berry muffins! Certainly we could—we should—try.

Since gold was discovered, San Francisco is becoming civilized at a rapid rate. However, it is not yet a place for ladies. I feared the danger was exacerbated by so many men possessing more time than duty, and vast amounts of liquor, with no ladies to draw them from evil doings. This may even put someone as well-intentioned as Edward in harm's way. He faces as much risk as any other. But, I must not allow myself to think thus. I will think only of the prime opportunity he is being given to help expand commerce to a new frontier.

<hr>

Wednesday, 6 July 1853

Edward travels back and forth between Methuen and Boston while I am in Salem assisting Miss Ward as an apprentice teacher this summer. I also still travel to Hamilton to occupy myself with my studies for several more weeks before I take a summer break. I am nearly qualified to teach a class of primary students on my own. I must complete my course of study, just as my beloved must seize the best opportunity to prepare for a prosperous life. We have vowed to wait patiently for each other and maintain a relationship of intimacy over the next few years even across a vast distance. We have promised to write each other weekly.

Edward is making note cards for me, so I will never be short of paper to write him. He prefers that I use an envelope rather than merely fold and seal my letter—he is constructing envelopes so we may retain the privacy of our messages.

CHAPTER 8

Love Before Work or Play

Miss M. L. Andrews
Care of Gen. Joseph Andrews
Salem
Masstts.

Methuen, [Thursday] 7th July, 1853

My dear Lizzie,

I have made inquiries about the mail from Lawrence to Salem and I find a letter from Lawrence reaches Salem at one P.M., and you will receive this just after school on Friday. I shall be on the lookout for your letters every Monday, and unless you think I am tasking you too much, be sure and walk part way home with Katy every Friday noon. There is one more piece of corresponding news I must tell you. If I go to San Francisco, we can have letters from each other once a week. For Mrs. Stephen P. Webb told me today she hears from her husband every week. This is Glorious, but I fear my pet may be disappointed; for it is doubtful whether I go to San Francisco for a year or two.

I received a letter from Uncle Edwin Bartlett yesterday, and he thinks it may be advisable for me to remain at Valparaiso "a year or two" before going to California. If this is to be for the best, I shall be much farther from you, and there is probably no regular communication between Valp. and the United States. But we must hope all will prove well and I shall feel that I must follow Uncle Edwin's advice to make sure of success.

Liz does not know when she will go to Maine. I shall do my best to hurry them away, that they (Liz & Mary) may return in season for your visit in August. I shall go on to New York the first of August to meet Uncle Edwin & Mr. Bissell, and I am to be ready for sea by the first of September. We must see as much of each other, between now and the 1st Sept., as we possibly can and avoid any unpleasant notices or remarks from other parties, like the discovery of Tuesday last. You have not heard anything more from that, have you? Don't be troubled if anyone should hear of it, for hardly any one would believe the story and even if they do, don't let it disturb you.

This morning I drove Coz. Mary Osgood to Andover to see Mrs. Webb of Salem, and I called to mind a drive to the same place two years ago with Coz. Mary & mother and you. You havn't forgotten it, have you? Emily Oliver was at our house then, for the afternoon. Wish you had been here today. When you see Emily, don't forget to ask what I shall do with her flower-basket. Perhaps I should send it to you and let you hand it to E. some time.

I have been very busy since I came from Salem and I ought perhaps to be working in the garden today; but though the adage is "work before play," my heart tells me "love before work or play," and this is the nearest approach to conversation we can well have when separated from each other twenty miles. How long an interval a week seems now. I dread to think of the months and years to come.

Sometimes I think I have done wrong to tell you of my love when I knew I must leave you for so long. For perhaps it may be a long time before I meet with any marked success in business and you know dearest, that I should not want to come home before I could tell you I had done something. Yet it could not have made much difference, for if we both loved each other truly, there was so much satisfaction in knowing the other's feelings, and there will now be so much more freedom and unreserved confidence in our correspondence. Now I feel that nothing can make me unhappy save the thought that you did not love me and that would I never feel. The very idea of such a thing was enough to twist my heart as it is very seldom wrenched, when we were so mistaken on Tuesday afternoon. Except with mother, at Father's death, I have not cried but once before for a long, long time. But then I could not help it; for the tears would come.

But it won't occur again, for my dearest pet knows she loves too well to wound my feelings. Have you missed me since Tuesday? I have missed you all the time. Be sure and write on Sunday and I shall receive your letter Monday P.M.

Good bye -
Edward

-----⊷⊶-----

Tuesday, 12 July 1853

I sat down at my writing desk and began to compose my missive to Edward. I must post today so he will receive it in Methuen on Monday. With all the secrecy about our letters, it is peculiar that Edward wants me to walk home with Katy Downing every week. Perhaps our engagement will be made public sooner than later.

Thank you, dear God, for the blessing that is Edward, for even the tragic loss of his father has not made him bitter. Instead, his tenderness has deepened. When he proposed we marry, I saw a tear in his eye and later asked him about it. He told me he could not help it. He has never loved anyone as much as he loves me. Had we not feared—each of us—that the other had gone away, perhaps we might not have realized our mutual affection. Certainly, neither of us would have experienced such joy and relief as we feel now.

⁓

Friday, 15 July, 1853

As Edward advised, I walked home from the train with Katy. We stopped at the post office and I retrieved a letter from Edward that had just arrived. I could hardly wait to reach my house and read it. I dared not peek until Katy departed toward her home.

As we walked, she told me she went to the Independence Day celebration in Methuen on Monday.

"Why would you travel to Methuen for the 4th of July when we have such a marvelous celebration here?" I asked.

"I have seen the Salem celebration before and, well..." She hesitated briefly before continuing, "Oh, Lizzie, do you not have any sense of adventure? Some days I simply want to burst out of my corset and ride on a man's saddle horse like a cowboy in a Wild West Show."

"Oh my, Katy!" I was a bit taken aback. "You are shocking!" I did not mean to offend her, so nervously continued, "I must admit I have none such desire. The performers in those shows seem to be odd birds to me."

"They are! Of course, but they are fearless. I want to try new things. I want to travel to new places. I went to Methuen simply because Liz and Edward told me I had an open invitation to join their family for a visit. So, I just went! That is why and that is the only reason. I do not regret it one iota. I had a marvelous time. You know, Lizzie, in these smaller towns, a lady from the city is treated a bit like a celebrity!"

She continued, "The celebration was small, with few skyward displays, but a most enjoyable picnic was organized—more than a dozen families brought twenty different pies. Throngs of children competed in races using gunny sacks and wheelbarrows."

Katy insisted I tell her all related to celebrations in Salem. I had

116

little I wished to say on the occasion, for that was the day Laura caught Edward kissing me. I could only think to tell her of the passing carriage that spotted me on the porch in only my bedclothes and my overcoat! After I told that story, we had a good laugh.

Katy assured me I could confide in her freely. She is very fond of Edward, and has promised him a report, but I think she must not recognize *all* there is to know about our engagement. I did, however, describe to her the horror that Edward and I experienced at the whim of my own sister interrupting our 'conversation' and the aftermath. That should satisfy her need to hear something about which she must remain ever so discreet. I did not tell Katy everything. I left her at the corner and walked home as briskly as my feet would carry me.

My conversation with her was one in a series of sensitive disclosures, which began two days after Edward was here for the 4th of July. First, Laura let the cat out of the bag. She failed to keep the confidence as Edward had requested of her. She told Father she wanted to go to San Francisco with Edward and Father inquired calmly as to why. She disclosed everything, including how she had seen Edward kissing me.

Father came to me and asked for an explanation. I confessed to my growing fondness of my cousin and my hope for a future with him, though I stopped short of disclosing our engagement. I assured him he could continue to trust us, for we had done nothing wrong. Father knew Edward intended to propose to me. He did not know it would be so soon. He was very sorry to think we could lose Edward to the frontier, and he could eventually lose me, as well—especially after Edward had worked so hard to complete his Harvard education and establish himself in Massachusetts.

I suppose it is not all bad that Father should know Edward's plans. I suspect he means to counsel Edward, for he does not know well the gentlemen who advise him. Father sees he has a duty in this regard, not only for my sake, but for that of my dear cousin. He has oft counseled me, speaking of the difficulty faced by ladies whose husbands have ventured so far from home, at times leaving a wife with child; perhaps, never returning to meet their own flesh and blood. They can simply disappear with no word. He knows Edward would never *intend* to do anything of the sort, but Father feels it his place to prepare me for the uncertainties and vicissitudes of life.

When I reached home with Edward's letter still unread, Aunt Eliza greeted me. I stopped for a few moments to speak with her before hurrying up to my room where I found a note included in the letter. I read the note first:

"Lizzie, my dearest pet, I think the greatest freedom in the world is to be known truly and deeply, and to be loved in spite of one's flaws. You must know I would risk looking the fool to confide my feelings in you and only you. At your request, I shall no longer aim to control what I say and or how I feel, but rather, I intend to show you everything there is to know about myself. Please meet me at Mrs. Webb's as we previously discussed. E."

I refolded the note and letter; then tucked them both in my diary under my mattress.

I must meet with Mrs. Webb to learn how she fares while her husband lives so far away. He was six months in Valparaiso before he ever reached San Francisco. How much better she must live as the respectable wife of a gentleman than if she would never have wed. It is not as if she is ever truly alone, for their hearts can meet through their letters.

As Mrs. Edward Tenney, my friends will know me as Lizzie Tenney or Mary Tenney. Either way, I will share a name with Edward's sisters until they marry! If I retain my family name of Mary Elizabeth Andrews Tenney, I could never monogram anything, for my initials would spell MEAT. Oh, conscience, this would never do! Perhaps I am destined to simply be M.E.—Mary Elizabeth, though I dream someday I might be M.E.T.

Then, I read his letter.

⸺⸺⸺

Emily Oliver with a basket of daffodils

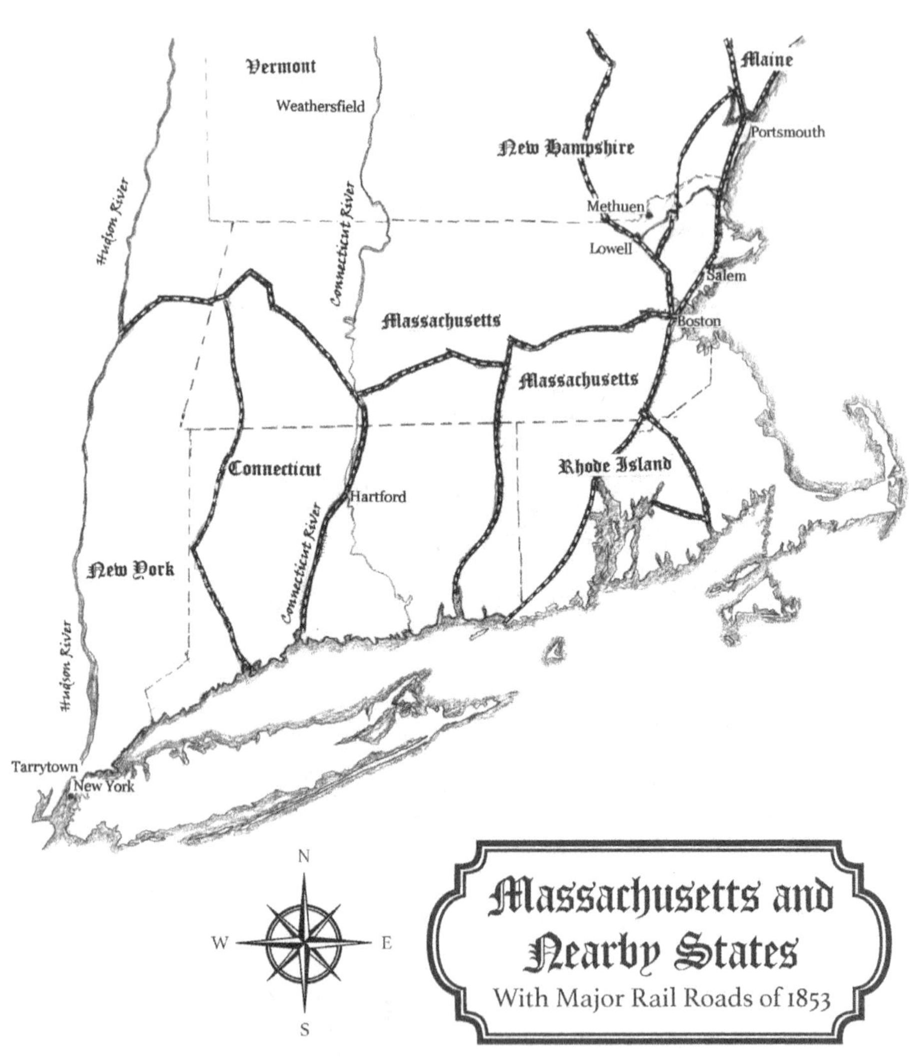

Vermont
Weathersfield
New Hampshire
Maine
Portsmouth
Methuen
Lowell
Salem
Boston
Massachusetts
Massachusetts
Hudson River
Connecticut River
Connecticut
Hartford
Rhode Island
Connecticut River
New York
Hudson River
Tarrytown
New York
N
W
E
S
Massachusetts and Nearby States
With Major Rail Roads of 1853

CHAPTER 9

Think of You Every Moment

Miss M. E. Andrews-
Care of Gen. J. Andrews
Salem
Mass.

Methuen, [Wednesday] 13th July, 1853

My dear Lizzie,

I will try the Lawrence mail once more and if you fail to receive my letter on Friday this time, I must adopt some new way of sending the rest. Or if you think best I will direct them to some fictitious address, say "Miss M. L. Tufts" (if there is no one of that name in Salem) or any other name. In that case you will have to ask on Friday "if there is anything for Miss M. L. T." This plan will not do, if the Post-master knows you, for he would suspect something wrong and perhaps report. It may be that I was misinformed by the Lawrence P.M. about the Salem mail, and if that be true there is danger of your father's or Joe's taking this letter from the office. At any rate if you receive this Safely on Friday, try and call at the office next Friday between 9 and 10 (if you can leave school) for the mail may leave Lawrence at 8 A.M. instead of at 12 M. So much for business; now for a little gossip.

Your letter I received safely on Monday P.M. and I felt very sorry for your sake to hear of Laura's awful disclosures. But I am glad nothing more troublesome was said. I shall expect another sheet next Monday, just like the last. Tomorrow morning I am going to Boston to return at noon, and I wish I could meet you there. We might call on Mrs. Tufts again after visiting Mr. Southard's.

Since Friday I have had as much riding as I wanted, free. Mr. Phillips (Margie P's father) had a present of a horse, chaise, harness, etc. from his father-in-law, but he had one horse, so he comes every day and asks me to exercise the new one. I am very glad of the chance. So I drive out with Liz or Mary or my dog#. Aunt Laur went with me yesterday. On Friday I am going to ride horse-back with four ladies, viz. Liz Tenney, Margie Phillips and two Misses Hubbard from Boston. I rather wish I hadn't more than two to look out for, but still I am sure of a fine time. You must learn to ride on horse-back, if you can.

Next Thursday (20th July) is Commencement and I expect to be in Cambridge Thursday and perhaps Friday. If so I will send my next letter from Boston or someplace nearby.

Mr. Briggs of Lawrence told me today that he met you in the Danvers cars not long ago, with "another lady not your sister." Do you remember it?

"The girls have not gone to Maine yet," if I ask Liz when she is going she says "tomorrow."

You think you can go to Boston and see the "Josephine," the first of your vacation; won't she sail again before August? Besides if you go up to visit the ship, your father and perhaps others will accompany you.

Don't your feet trouble you? I think they will before long; why can't you think so? Then you will have to call on Dr. Funnypasture. Any moderate degree of deception is allowable under the circumstances because if people will be so curious and gossiping they must be deceived in some way.

I hardly expected Mr. Whittemore would have called upon you so soon after the semi-cut of Class-day. But I hope he will not call again. Will he not be likely to come to Hamilton when his cousin Katy visits you? Don't for the world mention what I told you (to K) about W. for it would breed trouble all round.

"There!" I have written a most common-place, newspaper corresponding, uninteresting sort of a letter: but I have written it by daylight. No one, should it be opened, would imagine to whom I was writing, or what I felt while I wrote. For I am so much afraid of my letters to you being opened before you receive them, that I am very cautious. Please don't scold me very hard for my penmanship. "Do I think of you every moment?" Every half minute. Good bye-

"Ned"-ward
Please give my best love to Lizzie Andrews, if it won't make you jealous, but to no one else.
(#) I have a black Newfoundland puppy I am training.

<hr>

Saturday, 16 July 1853

I am tempted to board the train next Thursday and go to Boston to see Edward's commencement at Harvard. It will possibly be the last opportunity for me to see him, but I have no other reason to go, save my love for my dear cousin. Aunt Augusta, Liz and Mary plan to attend, but Father cannot, so there is no entourage from Salem I can join. My family's summer plans have come in the way. If my vacation would have been sooner, I could have boarded that Boston train. I may have no reason to visit Harvard in the future either; now that both JW and Edward have completed their studies, unless of course I have a son someday who might grow to follow in his father's footsteps and attend Harvard. *Heavens, this cart has gotten ahead of the horse!*

Edward is remarkable to have accomplished what he has, while also being pulled to fulfill his duty to his family. He will make a wonderful husband and father. However, once again, that is so long away! For now I must be content with him as my wayward Ned-ward, and I as his own dear pet.

Being each other's pet is the most silly of all sentiments. When Edward calls me his pet I understand he conveys the fullest expression of all he has shared with me—which, of course, he could not write in a letter or we might risk exposure. If we can maintain our secret, then no one will dissuade our frequent contact. There is no reason for us to be apart. Edward is honorable and would do nothing to taint my reputation, though I myself can hardly stop imagining how intimate our marriage might be. Oh dear! For now, I will be content to do little things for him.

I have assured Ned I will take Emily her basket. Any small favor will bring me pleasure.

Father says Joe may escort me to see *The Josephine*, the first of my vacation. Truly, my brother will love such a venture, and Father is more inclined to let me travel if we go together. Joe and I have been getting on finely. He has been coming to afternoon tea and remains very pleasant to all concerned. I suspect he is setting his sights on a course of action aboard *The Josephine*. He and Ned have conversed extensively of late, and I expect my time with Joe will allow him to reveal his plans. He dreams incessantly of sailing, and has quizzed Father on the challenges he might face should he go to sea. Father is encouraging him. It will be a splendid trip to take with my brother and, despite Edward's well-intended suggestion, I do not need to present Father with a falsehood, such as needing to see a doctor for my feet!

CHAPTER 10

Fear You Are in Danger

Miss M. E. Andrews
Care of Gen. Andrews
Salem
Mass.

Methuen, [Wednesday] 20th July, 1853

Dear Lizzie,

I am as impatient as I can be for your vacation to begin, for it seems months since I saw you, though only three weeks have passed. Laura came from Salem today and she says Miss Ward's school continues till Monday Aug. 8th, more than a week longer. Of course you will go to Boston as early in the week as you can (conveniently) and we ought to make some arrangement for meeting etc. Will my plan of meeting as acquaintances at "Southworth's & Hawes'," answer? If it will, send me word in what train you leave Salem. We will spend the necessary time at "S & H's" and then call again at Savin Hill if you are willing.

Oh Lizzie! Why can't you go out to San Francisco with me? We ought not to be separated from each other so far & so long. It seems as if I loved you so much that I shall be fit for nothing so far away, and I know your love for me is as strong as mine.

These last three weeks have made me feel almost discouraged at the thought of the years to come. To become accustomed to the separation will be impossible. Each week will increase the desire to be with you and I have no idea when I shall come home again. But it is foolish to brood over this. If I do right I shall prosper, and my success is yours. What treasure will be those weekly letters of yours. They will be my greatest comfort, and when you leave school I expect you will be writing all the time.

I have almost a foreboding tonight that you are in danger, for when I try to write I keep wishing you were in place of my lamp that I might put my arm around you and never let you go again. Remember and tell me what you were doing Thursday eve, at 10 P. M. When I see you in Boston, we will make some arrangement by which I can spend a Sunday at Hamilton before you come to Methuen and then I will call once more before leaving home. I will some time explain to you that sentence in my last letter you don't understand (?) since you ask me to. You haven't any objection, have you?

Oh dearest, I wish you were here tonight. Won't you try to imagine your head resting upon my shoulder? I often do, but you know I am too sentimental. Liz and Mary will not go to Maine till September, after I am gone. We have had one ride on horse-back since I wrote you, but that one has stopped all I expect. Last Friday the Misses Hubbard, Margie P. & myself started, after promising Mr. Phillips to return early. We called on Johnny Phillips in Andover and reached home at 11½. Mr. P. was very much frightened and says Margie shall ride no more till her mother comes home. So my pet mustn't be jealous any more. I am going to teach you to ride when you come to Methuen, and if you like it you must persuade your father to let you ride at the school in Boston. There is one Lizzie Andrews at Mr. Disbrow's riding-school now, a sister of "Spooney Andrews" of my class.

I received a letter from Uncle Edwin this week and I shall

probably not go to New York till September when I sail. I was sorry that everything could not be settled before leaving New York, but it was impossible, and I shall not know whether I am to stop at Valparaiso or go on to San Francisco, till I reach "Valp."

Does my pet take good care of herself? She must not eat green apples. Mr. Tufts didn't allow Ruth to eat them. Do you remember the instance? I am going to buy a magic cap by which I can make myself invisible and be with you every day. Does Pet ever grow tired of my long letters? I know she doesn't, why did I ask? Write by Monday. One kiss and good night, beloved -

E-

Saturday, 30 July 1853

Edward was so kind to escort Margie Phillips to visit her brother Johnny in Andover. I must not feel jealous of how generous he is with his time and affection, for those are the very attributes that draw me close to him. The thought that any mention of Lizzie Andrews turns his attention to me pleases me, even when the Lizzie Andrews at question is not me, but a sister of "Spooney" Andrews, not even part of our family.

What danger could Edward fear was facing me? I am either safe at home, at Miss Ward's, or at the post office. On weekends, I have little time for leisure. My activities typically do not bring me into danger.

I long for my holiday, which will not arrive for two more weeks. Then, I plan to take a good long one. I would gladly face the danger of travel to Boston were my reward to be a visit with Ned.

What was I doing on Wednesday eve, July 20 at 10 p.m. while Edward wrote to me? I was deep in slumber at that time so must have been dreaming of my Ned, as I often do. My sister Laura was most likely still awake at that time, engaged in a good long visit with his sister Mary at the Tenney home in Methuen, which they so often do when first reunited.

During the week, our home is quiet and dark by 10 p.m., when I usually retire for the night, for I must be at Miss Ward's by 7 a.m. to prepare for the students' arrival. I am often the first to sleep, while Father is typically the last, as he finishes his late-night reading.

By the time Friday arrives, I am eager to grab my satchel and parasol, bid good-bye to Miss Ward's and head down Chestnut Street to the post office. Since I have returned home from class-day three weeks ago, I have fabricated a clever excuse to go to the post office each Friday. I assign the girls to write letters to practice their penmanship. They must write a note to an aunt, uncle, or perhaps a cousin. One week I suggested they compose invitations to visit Miss Ward's School to join us for afternoon tea, and followed that the next week with a delightful session in which they practiced their skills at pouring and serving tea. Then, of course, I command they prepare notes to thank those who attended.

This requires regular trips to the post office for me, but it is no trouble at all. I tell Miss Ward I am happy to do it. If she could only know how happy, for along with posting letters from the girls, I include one from me to Edward and pick up a letter from my beloved. I assured Father that he need not trouble himself to inquire of the postmaster for Friday's mail, as it is now a convenient duty of my position as an apprentice teacher at Miss Ward's. That saves me the trouble of having Father review my own correspondence.

This Friday, as I walked, the thick summer air clung to my garments and with every step my corset slipped and resettled. I worried that my laces had become loosened with all the bending and stooping I had done over the pupils' desks that day. Walking was a welcomed activity, though the heat—and a slipping corset—made a vigorous walk potentially unsightly and therefore out of the question.

I crossed Chestnut Street and strolled by Hamilton Hall to see if preparations had begun for the dance the next evening. Not a speck of activity could be seen until I rounded the corner of Summer Street. Boys and young men streamed toward me in pairs and small groups and I could see that the Latin School had let out for the week-end. Their conversations had an edge of excitement to them, though everyone fell silent before passing me on the street. A few of the bolder ones greeted me with a simple, "Afternoon, ma'am."

I nodded acceptance of their greeting, however, I could not imagine when it had happened—when had I moved from 'Miss' to become 'Ma'am'? I felt no older than they; however, at eighteen years of age I was as much as eight years older than some, and likely two years older than even the oldest. Why, I was old enough to be married!

I assumed the posture of a married woman, dignified and confident, as I walked to town to begin preparations for my future husband's voyage. Certainly there must be a way I could become Mrs. Edward Tenney sooner than three years from now, if in fact his journey does indeed return him to New England as soon as that. Such a long absence will be difficult to endure.

I expect to continue my duties of teaching, if that is what I am called to do. Though, I have not the patience that a good schoolteacher must have. That was proven to me this very day. Just an hour before I departed, Miss Ward had words with me. Her voice echoed through my memory as I stepped from the dusty roadway onto the wooden walk on High Street.

"Lizzie, you are quite capable of stimulating the pupils to perform at their best. However..." that word rang in my ears, "...you must remember that they learn slowly until they have grasped the basics." Miss Ward was gentle but to the point. She says I must allow the pupils sufficient time to think through their answers before I offer a correction.

When I opened the post office door, it creaked and alerted the postmaster of my presence. He turned toward me and stepped to the counter.

"Good day, Miss Andrews. You are early today."

"Am I now? I suppose the students were eager to begin their weekend and completed their letters rather promptly." Perhaps my looking over their shoulders had indeed pushed them to that accomplishment.

He looked at me without comment, as if I had not just spoken. I handed him the packet of letters and averted my gaze, but continued to speak, "May I have mail for Miss Ward, General Andrews, Miss M. L. Tufts and … Miss Lizzie Andrews, of course."

"I believe I can help you on all counts, except there has not been any to Miss Tufts."

If such a letter were to arrive I must be sure to find it. The postmaster bundled more than two dozen letters together with a string, including a large packet for Father. I watched to see if I might recognize one from Edward, but his fingers moved so quickly, I did not spot such a letter.

"Is there postage due today?" I inquired, hoping to slow his activity.

"Not today. You must be doing a fine job with your teaching, Miss Andrews, for every letter to your pupils has been prepaid by the sender."

"Thank you, Mister." I let my voice drift off, for I realized I did not know the proper way to address the postmaster as I had never inquired of him as to his surname.

He completed my faded sentence. "Mr. Peterson, if you please."

"Mr. Peterson," I repeated. "Thank you."

I took the packet and tucked it in my bag. "Good day now." I smiled and turned to leave, eager to browse through the letters. I stepped outside, my boots clicked along the walk like a pendulum counting the moments until I could free my love message from the confines of the bundle. Once I rounded the corner, and saw that no one was watching, I fanned through the corners of the letters with a gloved finger, quickly spotting a familiar looking envelope. It was among only a few envelopes and stood out from the folded sheets of paper secured only by wax seals. I eased it from the strings, folded it once again and tucked it in my sleeve. The paper touched by Edward was now close to my skin. I could hardly wait to unfold the leaves and enter his world, for he was once again near to me.

As I turned onto Chestnut Street, my thoughts returned to Miss Ward. She is a spinster schoolmarm, with the patience of a saint. I am not like her, for I go utterly mad with boredom simply waiting for the pupils to respond to an inquiry. They slump in their chairs, chins stretched forward like chickens, and gaze about, as if the answers were floating above their heads. I am no better than they at maintaining my focus, however; for I watch the calendar all week until Friday, and then I begin to watch the clock! The pendulum simply demands my attention as it ticks off the minutes until I may slip out. I have done my best as an instructress, though, as I have learned today, the patience required for such a position is not an inherent virtue of mine. I would prefer to be at the side of my beloved Edward, for having patience is easy in that position.

Miss Ward's is quiet, and no one responds to my knock at the door, so I announce my entrance and step inside. I set the small bundle on her desk. Edward's letter rustles in my sleeve. My duties done, I hurry home to the privacy of my room where I can free Edward's letter from my sleeve and read.

As I step outside, I see Whittemore approaching me quickly from the direction of Cambridge Street. Perhaps he is on his way to see JW.

"Lizzie Andrews. How nice to see you. Are you headed home?"

"Yes." I say, not wanting to wait another moment to read Edward's letter.

"May I speak with you?" he asks.

"Certainly," I say, hoping we can complete our conversation in short course, knowing that were we to be seen together, misunderstanding of intentions would be possible.

"How are you this fine day?" he asks.

"I am well." I say, hoping my brevity will discourage any romantic intentions. I wait for him to speak. He looks around, but remains silent, and I wish to be alone with the letter scratching inside my sleeve. "Was there a specific matter about which you wished to speak with me?" I ask, maintaining as relaxed and pleasant a tone as I could muster.

"I am spending this week visiting in Salem." he begins. "JW tells me that there is to be a dance at Hamilton Hall tomorrow evening."

"Yes, I have heard as much."

"I would be honored if I might escort you to the dance, Lizzie."

"Of course. Laura and I are planning to attend. You may escort us both, if you wish." Oh, that I might tell him I am secretly betrothed.

"Fine. Shall I come for you at seven then?

"Seven? Certainly," I replied. "I shall bid you good-bye, then, until the morrow."

Salem Harbor

CHAPTER 11

Meet Accidentally

Gen. Joseph Andrews

Salem

Mass.

For Miss Lizzie Andrews

Methuen, [Thursday, P.M. 9 o'clock] July 21, 1853
[postmarked July 22 Boston]

My dear Lizzie:

I have just returned from Cambridge so tired that I should postpone till tomorrow anything but your letter. Commencement was on Wednesday and I left home Tuesday noon. Tuesday afternoon and evening I was running round Cambridge and Boston till after midnight preparing for the morrow. Wednesday morning at 9 o'clock commenced the exercises of the day and I was employed steadily till about 5 P.M. Then I spent an hour with Carrie Wilson and I was occupied till about 8 with gadding about. I then went to the President's levee for a short time and at 9½ walked a mile with the class to attend the parting class-supper, which began at 10 P.M. The class remained here from 10 till about 5 the next morning and had a fine time.

But I was ill and obliged to go to my room before half past ten. I was very sick all night, but today I have been on my feet the whole time.

Tomorrow morning I am going to Cambridge again, and perhaps on Saturday to dispose of my room's contents, bid classmates good-bye etc. I shall probably drop this letter in the Boston post-office, but I hope you will receive it as soon as if sent from Lawrence. Be sure and write on Sunday, for I may be called to New York on Tuesday for a week.

Mary said tonight that she and Liz were going to Maine next week to be gone a fortnight, so that they will be at home by the middle of August, which is in your vacation. I shall see you in Boston before then, won't I? Do come as soon as you can & send me word a day or two before-hand, that I may write you about the rendezvous &c, and whether I am sure to be here myself, for I shall have to go on to N. York the moment I receive a summons from Uncle Edwin. I should think the better plan would be for us to meet accidentally as common acquaintances at "Southworth & Hawes" on Tremont row, if there is any chance of your having company from Salem to Boston. If I spend a week in New York I will write you from there and Laura will suppose you have a letter from Kate Pollard.

Do you remember my "lapsus linguae" in Emmerton's room one class-day about "Salem beauty and the witch?" I had worse trouble yesterday. Some time ago I told Wilson that Carrie W. was said to be a great flirt, and Wilson in scolding C. for something repeated my remark to her. She told me of it yesterday and asked me why I said so. I cleared myself as well as I could and gave Wilson a scolding for telling C. and the result was that he became huffy and was very cross with Carrie. She fired up, naturally, and asked me to wait upon her home from our room. I consented, of course, but succeeded in reconciling the brother and sister so that Dave walked home with her. I met her in the cars today and all was good as pie.

Last Friday, as I wrote you, I rode horseback with four (girls) ladies, and we had a fine time, riding from six till nine. I promised to go whenever Margie P. wishes to ride and as I have been absent all the week we shall probably make the same party of five for tomorrow evening. I wish you were here to enjoy it. I wish you were here at any rate, and even if you did not ride horseback, I think you would enjoy yourself, would you not?

I don't object very much to your showing my letters to Lizzie Andrews. Did she seem pleased when you gave her my best love? Ask her if she don't wish we could see each other very soon. Will you take the best care of her, and see that no one is rude to her? Give her my bestest love again and _____ her so nicely for me. If you will do all this I will thank you from the bottom of your heart.

Good-bye, dearest, for a short time -

E

Sunday, 24 July 1853

Laura and I sat in the garden waiting for Father to pull the carriage around to take her to the train. I was trying to recall Edward's "slip of the tongue" in James Emmerton's room at Harvard when I must have uttered something aloud, for Laura spoke up.

"Pardon me?" she asked.

Realizing my own lapse of attention, I said, "You are fortunate to have this free time, Laura. I am certain you will enjoy your week in Methuen with the Tenneys. Have you packed your riding habit?"

"Yes, I have. Mary is anticipating several good long rides together. Lizzie, would you like to come along? Cousin Liz is home and I am certain she would enjoy a visit with you. We could help you fashion a riding outfit."

"You know I cannot leave yet, for I am obliged to teach two weeks hence at Miss Ward's. Thereafter, I am in Hamilton to make arrangements for my studies in September."

"Why must you study so hard, Lizzie? Father treats you as if you were his son!"

"I have thought as much, to be sure, but I do not blame him. He wants what is best for each of us. I do fear, however, at times I am too eager to satisfy Father for his loss of confidence in our brother."

"Shhh! He approaches." Laura warned, as she rose from the garden bench. Joe approached us and we quickly switched to converse on more mundane matters. "Laura, have a wonderful holiday. Be sure to give my best to Liz, will you? Kiss Aunt Augusta and all the rest for me." I followed her toward the street and she climbed aboard before Father could reach her to assist. Laura waved as the carriage disappeared into a cloud of road dust. I made my way into the house.

Upstairs, I situated myself at my desk and pulled Edward's last letter from under a book. The sheet crackled as I flattened it against the cherry wood. I wrote my weekly response imploring Edward to make a visit soon, as I would be unable to do so myself for some weeks. Perhaps we could meet in Hamilton where we could enjoy a pleasant walk, or better yet, in Salem, as it would be most gentlemanly were he to accompany my sister home on the train at her visit's end. I folded my message and prepared it for the morning's mail, pressing my seal into the amber wax. That marked the start of my wait for his next letter, or perhaps for his person to appear.

⁘

Thursday, 4 August 1853

I was most discouraged when Laura arrived *sans cousin*, after her week with the Tenneys. She charged into my room unannounced, and flew past me carrying something, as I readied to sit at my writing desk. She nearly startled me to death.

"Laura!" I shrieked. "Whatever has possessed you? Have you lost every bit of your manners during your stay in the country?"

She stammered and began toward the door. Then, without so much as an apology, bolted forward and slapped something on my feather bed. "I wanted to look under the seal, Lizzie. I could barely contain my curiosity —ever since I saw you and Edward…"

"Shhh! Laura, now hush. Why do you speak so? You were completely mistaken in your assessment of our encounter that day. Must I explain again that our intentions were as pure as any two cousins bidding farewell. To think any differently is sheer foolishness!" I chastised her just long enough to mask my own temptation to lunge at the object she laid upon the quilt.

"Methinks the lady does protest too much." Laura said.

"Laura, if you'd spent as much time with Shakespeare as you have with your *Godey's Lady's Book* you'd know the correct quote is, 'The lady doth protest too much, methinks.' It is from Hamlet. Certainly you have read Hamlet."

"What is it you have brought me?" I asked calmly, instantly forgetting Shakespeare.

"It is a parcel from Edward," she said smugly.

"Oh." I feigned disinterest.

"Are you not eager to open it?" she asked.

"I will open it in due course. At the moment I am writing to Kate Pollard, and I wish to finish my letter uninterrupted. You really must learn to knock before you enter, Laura."

"I am sorry, Lizzie, but Edward seemed quite intent that you receive this as soon as I could deliver it to you, and I just thought…oh, fiddle. I do not know what to think."

"As I can plainly see!"

I pushed my chair away from my desk and stood. "Laura, if you give me but a moment of privacy, I can finish my letter. Then, I will join you in the parlor to talk about your trip to Methuen. I expect it was most pleasant. Now, hurry off and I will see you in a moment."

"Of course," Laura sulked out of my room. I closed the door behind her.

When did I become so ruthlessly deceptive? Writing a letter to Kate Pollard! My word, I fibbed to my own sister. I guess I must now do as I say. Gathering Edward's parcel from the bed, I returned to my desk, set the package to the side and hastily scratched the date and two words onto a fresh sheet of paper.

"Dear Kate," Okay, it is begun.

Now, what has Edward sent? He does not possess a book of mine. I pulled the strings and broke open the seal. *Dream Life*, the title read. I turned the cover to find a note and a daguerreotype. Of Edward

Lizzie embroidering

CHAPTER 12

Dream Life

Miss M. E. Andrews
Methuen, [Wednesday] 3d August 1853

My dear Lizzie,

I send you "Dream Life," because my dream life has been somewhat like it. To be sure I have not met "Laura Dalton," but I have found my "Madge," long ago. You won't object to accepting it, will you? For it has been a pet book of mine, and if you can find time to read it before we meet again, we will compare notes. I should have marked some passages that were particularly striking, but I feared other eyes than yours (I mean my eyes that you keep for me) might notice the marking. I have told Laura that I was going to send by her a book that belonged to you, and she has been trying to find which one it is.

If I pass a Sabbath in Hamilton soon, I would rather choose one when you had no company, but how can I be sure of that? Laura says if I will be in H. the 14th, she will have Katy Downing out: but I don't want that.

But it won't be long before I see you in Boston, though a single day seems an age.

I write this just before L. leaves in the cars, to explain my returning your book, and I am "very much obliged" to you for the use of it. You will see that "Clarence's" life is not just like mine but there is some resemblance, and I know you will like the book.

You will tell me in your letter, which I shall receive Tuesday morning, what day and in what train you will go to Boston, won't you? I suppose you will receive my letters without trouble Friday noon.

Good bye till I write again.

Your E.-

———•⌘•———

Saturday, 6 August 1853

Laura is encouraging Edward to pursue Katy Downing! Goodness me. Katy seems to see Edward more than I see him of late; and I seem to see Katy more than I see Edward. I must tell Laura some compelling reason Katy should *not* come to Hamilton to meet Edward! My visits with Katy are quite pleasant as she is quite the conversationalist. In fact, she will talk to a perfect stranger as if she has known him for years! She did so in the Danvers cars the day we met Mr. Briggs. He seems to have a similar style and confidence as Katy, so it is no surprise one day he is rewarded by a young lady's admiration and another day he is snubbed.

It is but a week and a half until I meet Edward in Boston, so I shall not expect a letter at the post office tomorrow. Rather, as soon as my students leave at week's end, I will occupy myself reading *Dream Life* and savor Edward's message through Clarence.

I turned the first leaf and read until the sun had set and I could hear people gathering downstairs for Thursday supper.

———•⌘•———

The next day, I had nearly reached the midpoint in *Dream Life* when Father called me to dinner. As he took his place at the head of the table, he patted the breast of his waistcoat.

"After we dine, remind me, Lizzie, that I have something for you." And, with that he said not a word more about it through the entire meal. Oh, how he enjoys torturing me. Could he truly be so utterly cruel?

When the table was cleared, Father reached inside his coat and produced a letter. "It is sealed in an envelope. It must be private," he said.

"Who is it from, Father?" Laura asked.

"It is no business of yours," he told her and passed it to me.

"Really, Laura, must you tease so? It is merely a letter from your cousin Edward," Father announced as the heat rose to my face. Upstairs, I read my favorite literature, my own dream life, mailed to me in cherished installments, and delivered in person by my tease of a father.

⁕⁎⁕

Lizzie with a love letter

CHAPTER 13

Live in Hope

Miss M. E. Andrews
Care of Gen. J. Andrews
Salem
Mass.

Methuen, [Thursday] 4th August 1853

Dear Lizzie,

It seems as if the end of your term would never come. When I was in Salem I thought it would be but a short time from then till we could meet in Boston, but these four weeks have dragged themselves out into four months at least. I am growing so impatient that you may prepare yourself for a call when you would least imagine I was coming. Don't start if you find, on opening some book at school, that I am hidden among its leaves. I wish that were only possible. Though I sent you by Laura a hurried note, you may not receive it before you read this, and so I will caution you before hand to open Laura's note by yourself.

Do you remember telling me of a most charming Mrs. Haliburton of Portsmouth? I was very anxious to remember the name, because I thought the same lady had been described to me by a young dentist of P. I forgot all about it till yesterday when this person mentioned "the lovely widow of Portsmouth." I asked her name. "Mrs. Haliburton," he said. So I was right in my supposition. Laura said you were going to Portsmouth and to Deer Island this month. But we will talk of that when we meet again, and perhaps plan some accidental(?) meeting in the cars on the way to Portsmouth.

As to next week in Boston, I will leave that entirely to your next letter. I will meet you where you think best. I wish I had not disappointed you last Saturday by being in the last train of Salem cars. Had I known you were expecting me I should have tried to come at least, and probably have succeeded. I wish, as you say, that we could be together every evening till I am gone, that we might talk as we can't write. I imagine you sitting by me very often but that is a poor substitute for reality. I think it shall be easier when I have something to look at, but I shall never be satisfied unless the real, living, moving pet is with me. Now, too, it seems so tantalizing, that when only a few miles separate us, we are in reality as far apart as if I were in San Francisco. For then we can correspond weekly as now. Yet I try to think all is for the best. Perhaps as "distance lends enchantment &c.," a long separation may make a meeting the more pleasant; though I can't believe I can desire to see you more than I now do. Duty leads me away from you against my will, but I can carry with me the pleasant consciousness that I am laboring for you as well as for myself, and if nothing else would keep me busy that would. Don't you wish all was over now? We are only 18 and 20 years of age and if we were both free, what a luxury it would be to love each other without any forebodings of the future.

What will you do, when I am gone? As for me, I shall be too busy to allow repining: but you will have to live (I wrote it love at first) in hope. I am tempted to find fault with myself for having ever given you an opportunity of loving me and so fixing your hopes on such an uncertain point as I am. But I am determined to do well and all say that a firm determination is all that is necessary. If I succeed the credit is all yours; if I fail I can only blame myself.

Do you think I am too prosy in my letters? I can't write like others: I always let my pen follow my mind without restraint and so when I am moralizing my letters must be prosy. I wish you were here and I would promise not to be prosy, if I could help it.

I have everything to say to you when we meet; very soon, I hope.

Till when - adieu -
Edward

If this is mailed at Salem, you will know that I have called for you at Miss Ward's school and been very much disappointed; for I have determined to make a bold stroke to see you.

Good bye.

I closed the leaves of *Dream Life* and set the book on my desk whereupon I noticed a sheet of stationery with the words Dear Kate. I smoothed the sheet onto my writing surface, dated the letter and began.

Miss Kate Pollard
New York City, New York
7 August 1853

Dear Kate,

Greetings of the day, my dear friend.

I so enjoyed our visit in New York last year. Now, seeing as I am a seasoned traveler, I am readying to embark on a holiday to Boston and thereafter north to Portsmouth. Have you been there?

If you have, please tell me what you enjoyed there. I welcome any advice on buildings or shops I might visit....

------- ✦ -------

When I entered the parlor, Father was reading the daily news bulletin.

"May I interrupt?" I asked.

"Of course, my dear. What is it?"

"I wish very much to arrange a sitting so that I may have another daguerreotype made of my likeness."

"You would, would you?" Father asked, inviting my justification for such an expenditure at this time.

"Yes, I thought it might make a nice gift for family, maybe for grandmother, or for you... or for Joe—to help him remember me, while at sea. Or, perhaps for my cousin Edward," I said softly under my breath.

"So, I assume Edward's sisters are doing likewise?" Father grinned. He must have understood me. Then he chuckled a bit too long for my liking and I could feel myself biting the corner of my lip to control its trembling.

"If I allow this, Lizzie, you must promise me one thing."

"Yes?"

"You must find a better display for your hands than wringing them, as you do now."

Relieved to hear his consent, I placed my hands over my face. "Would this do, Father?"

"You are something else, Lizzie," he laughed. "You may make the arrangements. Request just two copies. Have the photographer send the statement to my office to be paid."

"Thank you, Father." I threw my arms around him. I am so fortunate!

My letters completed, I posted them Monday morning and was only a few minutes behind Miss Ward in preparing the classroom before the girls' arrival.

Tuesday morning I had my likeness made and requested a copy be sent directly to Edward. I planned to tell Father immediately that I had sent a copy to Edward already. I knew I should have waited. I should have brought both copies to Father first, but I simply could not make Edward wait.

When I reached home that afternoon, Father told me little Frankie Allen had passed away over the week-end. He was gone. His life ended too soon. I had held him in my arms not two months prior.

I cried for his mother. How does one survive such tragedy, losing a husband and a son in so short a time? I think there is nothing that can soothe the pain of losing a child so loved and so innocent. I cried for his sister Mamie.

The next few days were shrouded with mourning. There was not a dry eye to be seen as family passed through Salem to provide whatever comfort could be offered to a grieving mother.

Of course, I never spoke to Father of sending the daguerreotype to Edward. It is not as though I had forgotten. Such a matter simply seemed insignificant in light of the sorrow we all felt from little Frankie's death.

The days crept by slowly.

I postponed my trip to Boston for one week. I thought Friday would never arrive. I longed for a word of comfort and reassurance from Edward. After such a bitter week, I did not think I had a tear left inside me until I read his letter.

Bad news in a letter

III. Death & Deception

Even the most prosperous and well-established New England families were not immune to tragedies. Accidents or childhood diseases were not uncommon and society had yet to make significant advances in medicine or public safety. In addition, Salem's population included many occupations related to its busy harbor. Families with sons or fathers as mariners were well-aware of the risks their loved ones took. Families came together to provide support so those remaining could move forward with their lives.

CHAPTER 14

Little Frankie Allen

Miss M. E. Andrews
Care of Gen. Joseph Andrews
Salem
Masstts.

Methuen, [Thursday] 11th August, 1853

My dear Lizzie,

I have just been in to see little Frankie Allen; he seems so calm and free from pain that it does not make me feel sad to think his life has gone. The little fellow has only exchanged a world of trial mingled with some happiness for one where his pleasure is sure to be unalloyed. His face tells plainly that it cost him no struggle to make the change. His spirit seemed to leave him as quietly as a young dove flying towards its nest at night.

But poor Aunt Laur. I have been talking with her. She bears the trial as calmly as she can; it is only one blow more and but one remains. She pressed little Mamie to her heart and hopes God will spare her the only comfort she has left. It is very sad to talk with a mourner. There is a feeling of loneliness one can't conceal that calls upon you for your sympathy and condolence.

It seems trying to you now that we must separate for a few years. What if that separation were to be endless! Oh, dearest, think what a void would then be left in your heart. If death must part us ever, I could almost wish that you might be taken first and thus be spared the long and lonely years of sorrow. But there is no need of borrowing sorrow for what is inevitable. We must part some time, to meet again I trust; but before that I hope we shall enjoy many years of almost perfect happiness. It is this hope in the future that makes me so anxious to be at work; for the sooner I am fairly engaged in business the sooner I shall be able to come home and prove myself more worthy of a darling pet who has joined her hopes of future happiness with mine.

If you only knew who it is I have to make me so ambitious to succeed you would say I am sure to do well. She loves me as well as I love her and she has perfect confidence in me. Oh! She is a darling. Yesterday I brought home her daguerreotype and I have hardly had it out of my hand since. It is lying open on my desk now. I wish you could see it. She looks so sweetly and so happy with her pouting lips just ready to whisper "do you love me, Ned?" I guess "Ned" does love her a little bit, and always will. Suppose you ask him the next time you see him.

I have been wanting to show your daguerreotype to all the family and to all my acquaintances in Methuen. But prudence forbids; for even if they do not know you, they might recognize you at church with me and so let pussy out of the bag. I am certain the girls will find me in my room some time with the dag. in my hand but I will see that they don't know who is there. I must leave this last page for business and will wait till the cars come in with Mrs. Allen, Caddie Fellows etc. Good-bye, pet –

7 ½ P.M.- Ellen Allen did not come till this evening, dear pet, though she was expected at noon. It seems that everything has not been arranged in Salem as we supposed and I am going

down in the morning train. Aunt Laur will be there at noon with little Frank.

If you receive this in season, can you not call at Sarah E. Stearnes' some time during the afternoon? I will be there till 4 1/2 P.M. in hopes of seeing you though I suppose it is very doubtful if you come to Salem in season as "Katy & Caddie" are with you. But if you do, we can have a nice tete a tete without attracting any attention, and arrange about your visit of next week. If I don't see you tomorrow please call for your letter next week on Thursday instead of Friday, so that you can come to Methuen on Friday. I will be at Mrs. Carlton's or at Sarah E's from 1 or 2 to 4 1/2 tomorrow P.M, if it is possible. Be sure and write on Sunday even if "Katy & C." only allow time for one word. My darling must have been very tired yesterday was she not? I hope to see her tomorrow- A kiss?

Ned - your own

Do you want to know my pet's name? It is "Ned's own", isn't it?

P.S. I add one line to explain a curious note I am going to send by express. I shall not go to Salem till 12 o'clock with Aunt Laur, and to insure our meeting I shall send by express a note from Sarah E. Stearns. I direct it "Mr. M. E. A." to deceive the express, and I have written it in a manner that you will not have trouble if any one else sees it. I hardly expect to meet you, and if I don't, be sure to call for the next letter on Thursday. I shall devour your letter Tuesday morning. But I shall never stop.

Good night, darling - Dream all night of – Ned –

Friday, 12 August 1853

This morning I informed Miss Ward of the sad circumstances surrounding the death of my little cousin Frankie. She asked me to work until the girls went home for dinner, and assured me she had no concern she could manage the girls' lessons that afternoon when they returned.

I left Miss Ward's and walked toward the train station. I told Father I would meet Katy Downing and Caddie Fellows at the station. It would not be a long walk with them to the Stearns' home, where the family would join Aunt Laur in her grieving. I wondered how the grief of a mother might feel to lose something that is truly a part of you. Surely a mother's loss is as tragic as that of an orphaned child, although her grief must be different from the grief of a child who loses a parent too early. When death intrudes, life changes. Mourning must take precedence.

I found an empty bench to occupy, eager for Katy and Caddie to join me so we might begin our walk to the Stearns' home. Edward must have arrived already with Aunt Laur and little Frank. My spirits were lifted as I anticipated seeing him. Aunt Laur had stayed in Methuen with the Tenneys for the past month. Clearly, she depended on Edward to help her bring Frankie's tiny body back to Salem this morning.

Katy arrived just as the train whistled in the distance announcing its imminent arrival from Chelsea on which I expected to find Caddie. The train screeched to a stop. I approached to see her barely able to remove herself and all her skirts completely from the car. Passengers behind her turned to other doors to depart, rather than wait. The porter had to help her off the train onto the platform. I could not help but laugh. Her expression was supreme, as she stood dusting her skirts and catching her breath. She certainly needed the assistance. She greeted me with a sweet kiss.

"I have arrived!" she said.

"You certainly have! I am glad the porter helped your skirts off the train!"

"Oh, Caddie, it is so nice to laugh. Our whole circumstance seems so sad today, losing such a sweet child as Frankie. I held him not long ago. Although he felt frail, I never imagined he might be gone so soon."

"Lizzie, it is truly so sad. Can one ever be prepared for such a loss? For the loss of any loved one?" she asked.

"I suppose not. Yet, somehow we manage to carry on. What else can anyone do?"

We walked together through the thick summer heat toward the Stearns' home. It seemed we had just mourned together as a family with the passing of John Tenney. The loss of this boy brought a different type of sorrow. As common as death is, still a child's death seems to go against the natural order of things. Our prayers can only help us feel grateful for the miracle and the sweet innocence of a child's life.

We arrived at the Stearns' where Edward and Aunt Laur had laid out sweet little Frankie amidst the flowers and candles. After exchanging respectful greetings, Mary Osgood called both Katy and Caddie toward the kitchen. I made my way to visit my dear cousin. Edward seemed upset. He whispered to me under his breath, "Mother!" I looked across the room to see Aunt Augusta speaking with Aunt Laur. I did not understand what his reference meant.

"I beg your pardon?"

"Mother has breached my confidence in her," he whispered. "I heard her speaking with Mary Osgood. I cannot even speak of it now."

By the end of the afternoon I understood, for Mary had passed a rumor of our engagement to Caddie; Caddie informed Katy; and Katy revealed as much to Liz. Oh, heavens! Liz continued to spread the rumor to Mary Tenney; and Mary let Laura know. My sister ultimately confirmed her suspicion, and confronted me!

"Do not believe rumors!" I reprimanded Laura. I was careful not to deny that the rumor was true.

If they must talk, perhaps we should at least give them something to talk about.

———— ⤬ ————

By Monday evening, everyone had left Salem. Edward's letter arrived on Thursday, as he promised. I picked it up and waited to open it in the garden at my house, which I came to regret.

"What are you reading, Lizzie?" The inquiring voice approached from behind me, and gave me quite a start. I folded the sheets to prevent his reading a word.

"I beg your pardon?" I responded to buy time and formulate a nonchalant response. It was my brother. He was encroaching on me to see what was in my hand.

"What do you have there, Lizzie?" he asked again.

"Just a letter from our cousin," I answered coolly.

"It must not be from Liz, or you would not fold the page so," Joe insisted. He leaned over the wicker chair where I sat. I could feel his breath on the back of my neck.

"Joe, please!" I said and attempted to brush him away with my hand. He grabbed my arm behind me and stretched it over my head.

"Joseph," I cried in protest.

"Why Lizzie, I thought you were giving me your hand so I might assist you from your chair." He let go just as Aunt Eliza approached, perfectly timed, as she always was.

"What *are* you two up to?" she chided as if we were children.

"I was just leaving," he said.

"Good riddance," I let slip, surprising Aunt Eliza by my response.

"Lizzie, I came out to inquire if you have had your tea yet?

"Not yet. Is it ready? I would be glad to pour it. May we take tea in the garden today? The day is so lovely. Is Father joining us?"

"Lizzie," Aunt Eliza said again, slowly, "Perhaps you might wait until I answer your first question before you ask another."

"Oh, of course. I am sorry." I fell silent.

"To answer your questions, Bridget said tea will be ready in five minutes. We must go inside. She will bring it. That would be lovely if you would pour, but just for us ladies. Your father is taking tea in town. Laura is out for the afternoon and as for your brother, well, he will do what he does and we shan't worry about him today. He is out of bed and dressed, so we'll call that progress."

After a short silence I dared to express my thoughts on the subject of my brother. "Aunt Eliza, Joe is 20 years of age and he has never even been to a dance with a lady. I don't think he has a bit of interest in ever marrying or having a family."

"Some men are just not suited for marriage, Lizzie."

I wanted to ask more about that. Certainly Uncle Daniel could have married but never did. He has a fine manner about him, not as unpredictable or unseemly as Joe. I wanted to ask why Aunt Eliza never married, but could not find a way to ask without appearing rude.

"Do you think some are just lucky to find love, Aunt Eliza?"

"I guess one is lucky to find love, Lizzie. I think also one can decide that love is not a factor in deciding to marry. Love is a luxury, Lizzie. Marriage, and the decision to have a family, is a commitment and a legal agreement between two adults and their families. Many such arrangements have succeeded finely without the luxury of love." I was struck by hearing love described as a luxury, first by Edward and then by Aunt Eliza. I had never thought of it as such.

"Do you think I will marry and have a family some day?"

"I expect so. Yes, I think in good time, you will be a charming wife and a caring mother, Lizzie, however, you do not need to rush the matter. You have time. Your mother was nearly 23 years old when she married your father."

"Aunt Augusta was nearly 24 years old, which was 20 years younger than Senator Tenney when they married."

"Why all these questions about marriage, Lizzie?"

"I suppose I am just curious. I am 18 years old and, unlike Joe, I have had suitors." Aunt Eliza appeared to hold back a smile.

"Have you a serious suitor now, Lizzie?" I hoped she could not see the heat rush into my face.

"No. Oh, heavens no. Not me," I protested, perhaps a bit too vehemently.

"You do know, Lizzie, a gentleman would seek your father's approval and his blessing before you would ever hear of such a proposal."

Bridget prepared a refreshing lemony iced tea just as Grandmother arrived to join us. Aunt Eliza assisted Grandmother as I stood to pour tea, carefully tucking my letter under the apron of my tea dress as I sat. The conversation took a turn to discussing Father's new shipment of silks arriving that day at the Salem port and the lacework that Grandmother was completing that would someday adorn a beautiful gown. Grandmother was nearly 80 years old and she insisted it was her fancywork that kept her hands from freezing up with old age.

Lizzie shares a letter with her sister Laura

CHAPTER 15

Breach of Confidence

Miss M. E. Andrews
Care of Gen. J. Andrews
Salem
Mass.

Methuen, [Friday] 19th August – 1853

My dear Lizzie,

Ever since I left Hamilton I have been brooding over Mother's breach of confidence in telling Caddie Fellows what she did, and I have hardly been happy a moment. The more I think of it the more abominable it seems to be. When I came home this noon I could scarcely be even civil to mother and my own sisters. Such a state of feeling is very wrong, and I should not express it to any one but her who is dearer and nearer to me than any mother or sister could be. I know it is not right to feel otherwise than kindly towards mother & Liz, and therefore I have resolved to allow time for reflection, and I shall not mention the subject till Sunday. Had I spoken of it to them today, I know I should have said many things I ought not; for it seems so very dishonorable to act as both have done that I can't think calmly of it. Next Sunday I will have a long explanation with them and make them think that they are entirely mistaken in thinking I shall ever "propose" to you. I can very truthfully say that I shall never offer myself to you, and I know it will not occur to them that there will never be any need of it.

Yesterday afternoon, as I had to wait an hour in Salem, I called at Mrs. Emmerton's. Mary Osgood was there, and in joking about my pet, they seemed to imagine we were already engaged. Still no one knows anything about it; so they may think as they choose. If my darling is satisfied and happy (and I know she is) I don't care a straw for any one's opinion. Besides I always like to have any one joke me about you; for then I praise you to the skies as if I was very anxious to leave an impression that I was very fond of you, which is the best way to disarm suspicion.

Have not 'Katy and Caddie' said anything to you since I left? I know they think we like each other pretty well, to say the least. I shall wish Katy was your sister while I am in San Francisco; for she always seems to take such good care of you and love you so much. How nice it would be, should your father give up house-keeping, if you could board with her. I should feel much easier if I could leave you so, than I shall in leaving you with Joe.

I feel a great deal happier now than I did when I began to write. Then I had been thinking all the afternoon of what mother had said; even when I took up your daguerreotype to calm my feelings, I would feel more enraged to think they dared to speak of you. Now it almost seems as if I was with my little pet alone, and we were talking as freely as we always do. Doesn't my darling wish she were with Ned? Do ask her and tell me in your next letter. It is five days before we can meet again, but they will seem five weeks.

I find that the Lawrence cars reach Salem at nine o'clock; therefore I will be at the Lynde St. house just before 9 ¼, and if you are not there, I will go to Chestnut Street. If you prefer to meet me at any other place, tell me in Sunday's letter.

Did you notice how I was invited to Mr. Downing's? Katy said "I shall be very happy to see you at our house next week, with Lizzie," as if she knew we were to meet.

I am going to Boston tomorrow and I will mail your letter there. Aunt Laur is going to Chelsea with Mamie to get the hooping-cough. Truly so, because Dr. says it will be better for her now, than any other time.

I wish I were in Hamilton to bid you good night-

Good bye, pet, from your own Ned.

Railway station ticket office

Wednesday, 24 August 1853

I readied to depart Hamilton on Wednesday this week, rather than Thursday. My studies were completed for the summer, and my preparations to continue in September were complete. I had a two week break from my studies. Early Saturday, I was off to the depot to board the train for Boston and meet Edward.

Saturday, 27 August 1853

The train lurched into the Boston station and Edward's eyes searched in vain as each car window passed. He could not see that I was poised to depart behind the conductor who stood ready to drop the step upon our arrival.

"Southworth and Hawe's?" I called to get Edward's attention as I stepped toward him.

"Why yes, ma'am. At your service." he said, as if that were truly my destination. He grabbed my bag and turned so I might slip my hand in his other arm while he led me through the crowd to his father's buggy.

"You have your father's carriage?" I asked.

"Yes, though I considered greeting you with two saddle horses."

"I expected as much! What with your desire to place me upon some unruly steed, I should not have been a bit shocked, but this…this, is a pleasant surprise." He helped me onto the bench, placed my bag behind me, and produced a blanket for my lap. The warmth was not needed today, but such a thing was necessary to keep my dress free from dust kicked up by the horse.

Edward climbed into his seat and snapped the horse into motion before he glanced at me and spoke. "Lizzie, I have looked so forward to our meeting that we must now slow each moment and savor it." The horse trotted along at a pleasant pace. The breeze carried a hint of crispness from the early morning air. "No one is expecting us in Chelsea until sundown, so we have time for a walk, if it pleases you."

"It would indeed."

We traveled to the edge of town toward Cambridge where the grasses and trees were enjoying the long summer days. Edward held my hand while he wrapped his other arm around my waist and we walked slowly until we found a path into the woods. Edward started down the path through the trees. It was cooler in the shade. Sunlight fell through the branches and speckled the ground.

Edward stopped and turned back toward me. "Look at the way the light falls on your skirt." He stroked the silk panel from my waist to my sides and then pulled me toward him. He pressed himself against me from cheek to toe. Oh, more than merely touching toes, he pushed his foot between mine forcing them to part enough to make room for his. Fearing I would otherwise lose my balance, I allowed my weight to give way and shift. Soon his large foot lay completely along the inside of my slippers, which were exposed and looked frightfully small surrounded by his hard leather boots. His knees pressed deeply into my skirts, the silk seeming to wrap itself around his impression. I will never know how my limbs resisted folding like a fan and depositing me on the ground, for I was nearly suspended and weightless in his arms. He wrapped them so completely around me that I was certain the whalebones in my corset would snap. His face felt smooth and warm against my cheek, until the tiniest move raked sightless whiskers against my skin. Before I could reach up to my face, he stroked my cheekbone with his thumb. "I'm sorry, Lizzie. Am I too rough for you?" His hand felt soft.

"No. Not too," I felt the tenderness of his touch but he seemed unaware of his own strength and I felt suddenly aware of what little strength or control I had.

"Edward, do not let me fall."

"You cannot fall, Lizzie, for I will never let you go, even after my arms have traveled around the cape." He whispered again in my ear, "I will never let you go."

I was lulled by the rhythm of his breathing, at first deeper and slower than my own, its pace began increasing. He tipped my face toward his and I looked into his eyes. I wanted to tell him that my heart, too, would wait the length of his journey, whether it be months or years, but before a word could leave my mouth his lips were against mine. My own, once pursed to speak, softened like summer butter yielding to the warmth of the afternoon. I grabbed the hem of his waistcoat and slid my fingers underneath. His shirt felt damp as I moved my hand against his back, hoping my touch could say what my words could not.

He took a deep breath and as he exhaled every part of him seemed to be folded into my skirts. Were it not for my corset and crinoline, I would have had no defense against his passion. Suddenly, he pulled back and nearly knocked me off balance. Turning abruptly toward the carriage, he swept my shawl from my arm, and held his elbow out for me.

"Lizzie, let us walk."

Somewhat startled, I reached for his arm and followed. "Of course, as you wish."

He continued, "It is a beautiful day and I want to see the lush countryside one more time before I leave – one more time before long, dry land will be a thing of my past."

We strolled for more than an hour, and as there was no need for a shawl on this sunny day, Edward carried it for me.

As we later departed, he asked if he might take my shawl to remember me and this day.

"Of course you may, but have you misplaced my daguerreotype? Surely that is a better reminder of my likeness than this shawl."

"I could never lose sight of that treasure, and I never want to lose sight of the day in which your beauty surpassed that of your own daguerreotype."

CHAPTER 16

Say Nothing of It

Miss M. E. Andrews

Care of Gen. J. Andrews

Salem

Mass.

Methuen, [Thursday] 8th September, 1853

Dear Lizzie.

I am in a most deplorable state of mind and body and am wholly unfit for writing; so you must excuse the substance of this letter. Yesterday afternoon I was attacked by the toothache, which has continued all night and now is torturing my poor head dreadfully. I could not go to the Dentist this morning, and I am to call on one in Boston this afternoon. I was intending to go to Boston today and leave for New York at half past five. I shall do this even now if my tooth is taken out in season. This idea of going to New York is something new, but I found I must talk with Uncle Edwin before I could go away. If I am likely to enjoy myself at Tarrytown, I may stay a week: if not I shall come home sooner. Be sure and write to me on Sunday as usual and direct to "care of Edwin Bartlett Esq. Tarrytown - N.Y." Uncle E. wrote me yesterday that "our steamer may not be ready before 1st November." Another month added to my stay in New England, for which I am very glad for our sake, but sorry to have the appearance of doing nothing at home.

Yesterday I had quite a long and perfectly frank conversation with mother. Of course the incidents of Sunday evening were called up and resulted in a promise from each of us to try and forget everything that had occurred. In order to convince Mother that we had done nothing wrong, I told her that tho we were not publicly engaged, yet we understood each other's feelings, -and moreover your father consented to the understanding now existing between us. Mother said she was very glad to know this; if she had known it before she would not have spoken as she had done. She promised to say nothing of it to any one, and to forget all the difficulty we have had. I do not think she will ever mention what I told her; but even if she should, it can not go farther than Aunt Mary or Laura. Do you think I did right or not? It seemed to me the only way to make a fair explanation with mother, though I should have preferred to talk with you before saying anything. Tell me what you think when you write.

Have you asked your father about your daguerreotype? I met him in Boston on Monday, dined with him and as he said nothing, I concluded he had not said 'no.'

I was very glad to hear that Joe is likely to go out in the ship soon. I hope nothing will prevent it. It will make me feel very much happier to think my pet is free from such a brother for a time at least. And it may prove a starting point to something better. I came very near opening your letter to Liz last Tuesday. I took it from the office and recognizing the writing, should not have stopped to read the address, had not my eye caught "Care of" &c. What if I had read it?

I sent a dog to "Grandmother's" today for your father. I was tempted to bring him down myself. Please tell Edward not to let him go into the house, not to give him meat for a long time, but bread and milk with Indian Meal thrown in. Excuse my troubling you with such commissions, but I could not help. I have every night thought of your request, and have seen you pretty often. I think we can pass two Sabbaths together if I stay till November, can't we?

Good bye - dearest –
Your Ned

Be sure & write on Sunday.

Boston P.M. I have had my tooth taken out and shall start for N.Y. at 5 ½. Be sure & write to me at Tarrytown. I have you in my valise "Good bye" --

I am very glad I have made up everything with mother. "Dear pet"

Saturday, 10 September 1853

I found Father in his office. He looked up at me and smiled.

"Father, Edward has sent you a gift to Grandmother Sprague's. Did you know he was doing that?" I asked.

"Yes," he said softly and gestured for me to come closer to him. When I did, and no one could hear, he said, "It is part of the bride price."

"Father!" I shrieked, which was the wrong thing to do since it brought attention to our conversation and Aunt Eliza came running to see what was the matter.

Father laughed. "It is nothing. Lizzie is very excited to hear we will be having a dog and that she is to care for it."

"I know nothing about properly caring for a dog, Father," I said to improvise an explanation for my sudden outburst.

"A dog?" Aunt Eliza inquired.

"A dog?" Joe exclaimed as he came into Father's office. With all four of us cowering over his desk, Father stood to usher us out so he might explain in a more comfortable setting.

"Yes, it seems Edward Tenney has become quite fond of dogs and has had some success at training them to fetch. He determined that a certain breed of retriever, a Labrador, rather than the smaller Cocker Spaniel, as had been suggested previously, would be most suitable for our household. It would be kenneled in the stable and would keep fine company to the horse. I am not sure what we would have it fetch but yes, Joe, he encouraged you to write him so he might tell you of his experiences. He suggested you might find entertainment in a game of fetch with the dog."

"And Lizzie is to care for it?" Joe asked in earnest.

"No, of course not. Edward Clark is to see to its food and water. He has had a dog before. Now that James has left, he will take on all the outdoor chores including caring for Bobby. I expect we will all find the dog fine company, as it will keep the squirrels from menacing us in the garden for an afternoon tea-cake! The dog is not to come in the house, however," he said and smiled wryly at Joe.

Rockwood Estate on the Hudson River

CHAPTER 17

Rockwood Estate

Miss M. E. Andrews

Care of Gen. J. Andrews

Salem

Mass

Rockwood, [Wednesday] 14th Sept. 1853.

Dear Lizzie-

I am enjoying myself so much here that I have no idea when I shall go home again. Uncle Edwin is the best uncle that ever lived and Aunt Carrie is a 'perfect love' of an aunt.

I reached Rockwood last Friday evening, after spending a day in New York, (breakfasting at 'Taylor's', and spending an hour in the Crystal Palace, roaming about the city, seeing the sights &c. &c.) Since I came here the hours have flown so fast that I have no realization of time. In the morning, after break-fasting, reading the papers, and taking a stroll on the farm, I play billiards with Uncle for two hours or longer, then read till din-ner. After dinner I talk or walk or read or ride, or examine the house. There have been some guests here all the time. Yesterday morning Commodore and Mrs. McKeever went away and before dinner seven from the Jarvises came to take their places.

Commodore McKeever has been a fine companion. He has kept me laughing the whole time. He has invited me to visit him in New York and I have promised to call. Yesterday morning I rode with him to the depot and found your letter in the Post-office, so that I have received it as soon as if I was at Methuen.

I wish I could give you some description of Rockwood (for so Uncle E's place has been named) but I could impart no idea of what it really is. Independent of what money and taste has done for it, I think there are few situations in the country which surpass it. R. consists of 200 acres on the Easterly bank of the Hudson, about thirty miles from New York & three from Tarrytown. Everything is yet incomplete except the house and stables. The flower-garden, a porter's lodge at the gate, the laying out of groves, walks etc. yet remain to be begun. The avenues for carriages are to be finished before anything else is commenced. The farm barn and stable are equal both inside and outside to many fine cottages in Essex County, Mass. As for the house, I know that I ought not to try to talk of that. It is an immense English stone castle of the "Elizabethan style of architecture," of the most perfect proportion and taste. Its estimated cost is over two hundred thousand dollars. Commodore McKeever assures me that it has no equal in this country at least nearly all the inside of the house has been imported from France. As I entered, the Hall (after dark) was lighted and I was perfectly startled by the magnificence. The flooring is far handsomer than any marble I ever saw, being formed of many colored octagonal blocks of I-know-not-what. Its size is enormous, containing sofas, chairs, lounges &c. on the sides. I was ushered into the library, and then the Hall seemed common-place in comparison with it.

The sides part of the ceiling, the fire-place are of black-walnut, beautifully carved. The ceiling is painted of different shades of blue and gold, the paper corresponds, (what little there is to be papered) and the room, is furnished throughout with the same perfect taste that marks every room in the house. The drafting-room is the most magnificent of course.

The carpet is one single piece made to order in France, and all the upholstery corresponds with it. The ceiling is of painted canvas. There is nothing gaudy or out of place in the whole house. The dining room is of oak finish, with a carved fire-place and bureau. Every room is entirely different from every other, yet perfect in itself. My room is the lilac room, where the paper, furniture and, everything correspond exactly. The 'Chintz room' is called the most darling and love of a room. As for accommodation, with all the strangers Aunt now has there is no one occupying the same story with me. I am writing this in my own room, to avoid the noise of those in the library. I have wished a dozen times each day that you were here to enjoy Rockwood with me. I have wanted to show Aunt your daguerreotype, but I know it will not do. So I keep it locked up but look at it once in a while myself. I want to stay here a long time but I am afraid of wearing my welcome out, so I think I shall return home next week. Direct your next letter to me at Tarrytown as before and be sure to put it in the office at the same time, for I may go home on Tuesday.

As for Valparaiso, I can not tell yet when the San Francisco will leave. Uncle E. has promised to write me as soon as he can ascertain. I am very anxious to know whether Joseph has gone yet. You make no mention of it in your letter. Of course I can not be in Hamilton this week, though I want to see you. But perhaps next week I can come. You must excuse my bad writing this time for I have but one pen and write on unruled paper. I am very glad your father consents to my having your daguerreotype and I long to hear what he said to you. Won't you treasure it up till I see you? I wish you would write me what to purchase for Laura.

Lizzie & Mary are delighted with their saddle, but Mother thinks I can't afford it. I have rattled on so fast that I have written a dreadfully long letter in a dreadful hand. Will you excuse me? I wish you could see Rockwood.

Good bye,
N.

———·⁂·———

Saturday, 17 September 1853

"Oh, Laura, you must let me read you my letter from Edward."

"You want to read Edward's letter to me? Lizzie, what has come over you? You told me what he writes to you is not my concern. And, you were not very nice about it."

"Oh, sister, I do apologize. I was wrong to be so unkind, but this one simply must be shared with someone."

Opening the letter would certainly show her my intention. I continued, "Won't you be a dear of a sister and sit with me a moment? Keep my confidence." Grabbing her arm and nearly dragging her down the hall, we settled on the settee in the corner of the parlor where we could be private yet forewarned of anyone's approach.

"Laura, Edward has been staying in a magnificent New York estate and has visited the Crystal Palace."

"What is the Crystal Palace?"

"Do you not remember what Father told us of it? New York has followed what occurred in London just two years past and opened our own Crystal Palace on Bastille Day. They call it "the Great Exhibition of Art and Industry.""

"I don't remember him saying anything about this."

"Here," I said, and went to the bookshelf to thumb through a stack of articles. "It's in here somewhere. Ah, here. Look. Read it aloud, Laura." She read.

"An Ode for the Inauguration of the American Crystal Palace by William R. Wallace, *New York Times*, July 14, 1853. The nations meet, not in war, but in peace, beneath this dome. They meet to bring glory to God on high and goodwill to men. The Crystal Palace is a symbol of the might of Man. Look on, ye Nations, and vow eternal peace and justice."

She spoke the words as if reciting a dull school lesson.

"Is that not splendid?" I inquired.

"What?" She appeared truly puzzled.

I tried not to let my impatience show. "An international exhibition that displays the achievements of the entire world! Laura, have you ever really thought about these times in which we live?" For two weeks now, I had been teaching students of twelve and thirteen years, not much younger than Laura. Miss Ward needed an assistant now that her school boasted two dozen young ladies. This allowed me to witness the manner in which Miss Ward questioned students. She was able to draw them excitedly into educational discourses. During the middle of each week, I traveled to Hamilton to continue my own studies, returning to teach at Miss Ward's the remaining days.

Laura's dull expression disappointed me and confirmed that I was no Miss Ward. Thinking of how Miss Ward taught, I began to move about the parlor to emphasize my message, "Progress is racing forward at a speed never before known to mankind. Our nation is honoring that progress at the Crystal Palace." This was as fine an explanation as any teacher could provide, but Laura remained uninterested.

"Don't you see, Laura?" Truly, I wanted to shake her. "Today, a young nation like ours can make a significant contribution to the world's new industries, as much as any country. All the world has come to New York to view each nation's achievements."

"Why don't you go there, Lizzie, if you care so much about it?" Laura asked.

Teaching may not be my cup of tea after all. It would suit me as a temporary vocation until I could join Edward. I responded, "Perhaps I will. It certainly does not seem right that I should be here while Edward is there."

"Edward is where?" Father's voice boomed from the hallway behind me and caused quite a start. He had planted himself in full view of my pedagogical display. Aunt Eliza and Joe stood just behind him.

"Heavens! You frightened me, Father. How long have you been standing there?" I asked.

"I saw you in the parlor and thought you might need assistance," Father said. "But it appears you are finding everything you need on your own."

"Well, yes, well … my knowledge is quite limited," I admitted.

Father crossed the room and pulled out another paper from the stack. Aunt Eliza followed Father and began tidying the pile. I motioned Laura to make room for me to join her. Joe entered the room and settled into an arm chair.

"Edward Riddle." Father read, as he settled into his chair. "Have you heard that name?"

Heads shook all around the room.

"He assembled several bankers from New York, after hearing their marvelous stories of the Crystal Palace in London and convinced them to invest in a similar venture in our country. Your cousin is among thousands travelling to New York for this purpose."

"May I see that?" Joe asked and was handed the papers. Laura had discovered a copy of *Godey's Lady's Book* and began flipping through the pages.

"Do you see where it discusses the design, Joe?" Father asked. "The man who created Tivoli Gardens in Copenhagen was one of the designers."

Turning the page over, Joe rose to his feet.

"How did they do that?" He yelled. "Look at that dome! It is colossal." He held the picture close to Father's face and began tapping on it excitedly with his finger. He marched over to Laura demanding her attention. "Laura, look at this! See how the arms are equal in length?" Laura cowered in her seat holding up her *Godey's Lady's Book* as if it were a shield. Father intervened, calmly taking control of the situation.

"What was it you were reading, Laura?" Father asked.

"I was reading *Godey's*, Father," Laura said sheepishly, and attempted to justify her inattention to the conversation at hand. "I thought I might find a pattern for a woolen shirt for Joe so he might be better prepared for the weather when at sea. A Miss R. L. is listed in the book as having ordered such a pattern. I think that must be Rose Lee! Do you not think so?" Laura looked across the room to me and continued to speak. "I may be able to use her shirt pattern and instructions when she no longer needs them."

"Laura. I am not referring to what you are reading at this moment." He seemed undisturbed with Laura's long-winded response. "I heard you reading about the Crystal Palace earlier," he coached. Laura closed her magazine and began reading the passage she had read earlier without a bit of inflection in her tone.

"The nations meet, not in war, but in peace, beneath this dome…"

Father interrupted, "That" he emphasized. "That is the purpose of such a building and such an exhibition – to help us learn from each other and work together on advancements that require contributions from all good minds. Yes, we have great industries emerging, but they can be the cause of much suffering in the world."

"Suffering?" I asked.

Father explained, "Working in our own nation's textile industry has caused hardship and even death for some workers, which is a great price to pay for the profits made by some."

"Doesn't our own family benefit from the labors of others?"

"We do, indeed, and that is why we must never forget the cost to others." He looked at me and continued, "You know Emily Oliver? Her father has been diligently committed to protecting workers in the mills. Due to this, he has been able to hire the best workers and has increased profits as a result. That is the spirit that built the Crystal Palace exhibition." He continued, speaking now to Joe, "Bosses must answer to both the owners and the workers whose labor creates the profits."

"Answer to the workers? The immigrants can be replaced." Joe was disgusted.

"Do you not think they should have an opportunity to benefit from their own labor and risk?" Father posed the question to us all, as if we were being schooled, but did not wait for a response.

"The factories in New York are a small consideration compared to serious challenges in the West and the South we do not see. Immigrant labor is building the transcontinental railroads and African slave labor produces the cotton in the South for fabrics made in the nearby textile mills. The nation's attention to the Crystal Palace is a positive diversion from the growing unrest between the slave owners and those who feel no man should have the right to own another."

"It is not like the slaves are civilized men, Father." Joe continued his disrespectful barbs.

"Joe!" I said in disgust. "They would certainly act in a civilized manner if they were educated as we have been! But then again," I jabbed, "look at what your education has done for you."

"That's enough, Lizzie." Father's voice was firm as he united us to focus on the Crystal Palace, motioning us to approach him for the rest of the lesson.

New York Crystal Palace

"Look at these columns. Each is seventy feet tall. The dome is the largest of its kind in the Western world." He paused and continued pensively, "Men have mastered architecture but not yet resolved our social ills. That, to me, is the greatest wonder of it all." Father paused and seeing no response, he stated simply, "Well, I see I have exhausted this lesson and it appears I may have exhausted you three, as well," he chuckled and slowly rose to leave, pausing momentarily as if to speak but, uttering nothing, turned and departed.

Joe huffed and stomped out after him, leaving Laura and me to ourselves.

"What are you going to do now?" she asked.

"Perhaps compose my response to Edward's letter. If posted tomorrow, he will receive it by Tuesday." I unfolded the letter I had been clutching in my hand. "I could read you the part about the estate where he is staying if you like.

"I would like that," she answered sweetly, perhaps yielding to Father's suggestion that we put as much effort into kindness as to our advancements.

The rest of the day was peaceful and fruitful and my letter was posted as planned on Monday.

My pet told me not to expect a visit for at least two Sabbaths. Much transpired in those two weeks.

Joe confirmed his plans to take a position as a crew member on *The Josephine*. Father says the first of my vacation I may have Joe escort me to see the ship. Truly Joe will love such a venture and Father is more inclined to let me travel there if we go together, as Joe and I have been getting on well now that he has set his sights on a course of action.

Teaching kept me well occupied with Sunday school and a full week at Miss Ward's. On Friday, my students are growing restless for the Sabbath break and no matter of interest keeps them in their seats for long. The sound of young voices call*ing* "Miss Lizzie" rang through my ears all day. At mid-day, squeals and shrieks emanated from the front door and I could see a gentleman had arrived in a white straw hat.

I'd seen such a hat adorning onlookers in the pictures of the Crystal Palace, but thought nothing of it—until I heard a chorus singing "Miss Lizzie." Students clamored down the hall to find me.

"Someone has called for you, Miss Lizzie!" said one.

"Yes, a gentleman," added another.

"With a dazzling hat!" giggled a third.

Miss Ward nodded and waved me off to attend to the visitor. I never expected my own pet to be standing in the hallway.

My skirts swept the floor behind me as I blurted my greeting, "My Pet!"

Edward held a finger to his lips shushing me to silence as students gathered like dust at my heels.

"Miss Lizzie," Edward opened his palm to accept my hand, tipping his white hat while the girls rustled about in excitement. We had only a few minutes to visit, so quickly took our conversation outside where I extended an invitation for Edward to join us for supper.

As I was called to return to the school house, Edward offered to pick up my post for me. "My letter of warning must be sitting there now," he said. "You really must check the post office on your way to Miss Ward's or she may never know what a white-hatted gentleman caller might have on his mind."

With students dismissed, winged feet carried me home. That place, which Edward once considered grand, would pale now in comparison with the extraordinary Rockwood Estate that recently provided him comfort. Instead of approaching a porter's lodge at the entrance gate, landscaping scarred with spent blooms greeted me. There was no gardener at the Andrews', no well-laid garden paths. Entering the tiny foyer, wall hooks took my wrap for me.

Among the furnishings sat Edward holding a note that had arrived mid-morning. His fresh face brightened any bit of fatigue from the room and from me. I joined him and he handed me a letter from him with a late announcement of his own arrival.

⁕

CHAPTER 18

Call for You at Miss Ward's

Miss M. E. Andrews
Care of Genl. J. Andrews
Salem
Mass.

Methuen, [Friday] 23d Sept. 1853

Dear Lizzie.

I can only scribble a few lines to you before the cars start, to send in case I don't meet you in Salem today.

I want very much to spend next Sunday with you, but I should not do so if you have visitors now, so I intend to call for you at Miss Ward's school at 12 o'clock today, unless I meet your father in Boston.

I did not reach home from New York till Thursday, so of course I was unable to be in Hamilton by the middle of week as you wished. It is time for me to go to the cars but I may write more in Boston.

If by any ill luck, I can't find you in Salem today, write me on Sunday what to do about coming to Hamilton. I feel sure I shall see you, however. So good bye for a few hours only,

Ned.

Friday, 23 September 1853

My reprimand about not writing was soon forgotten as supper led to a convivial and entertaining evening with Edward's stories of New York and Rockwood.

Father spoke of going by boat to Saint John, New Brunswick and bringing Joe with him. Father expects a shipment of silks to arrive mid-week and is arranging passage for the two of them to continue on with the ship to Halifax. It would be a brief stop returning to Salem the next day. Joe will have an opportunity to watch a seasoned crew before he is to ship out for the first time. He is looking forward to getting his sea legs. Father seems cheered by the opportunity to more fully prepare Joe to join the crew on *The Josephine*.

Edward was too soon off to catch the last car to Methuen, leaving me to count the days until his next post, which fortunately arrived in less than a week. Before he departed I told him of the presents I was making for him. It had been some time since I fashioned his slippers, and certainly this would be something he needed while he was away. The matter of warm woolen socks was also discussed and both his sister and I were working diligently to make socks with tightly knit stitches that would keep his feet warm and dry. There was one more surprise. I almost kept it to myself, but as he turned to depart, it provided me one more reason for prolonging our moment together.

We stepped off the porch after the lamplighter passed, remaining silent as the lamp was lit and the lamplighter lumbered down the street attending to his daily task. Early evening shade began to define the circle of light that fell from the lamp onto the cobblestones. Edward pulled me toward him, reassuring me, "There is no one about."

I scanned for myself to confirm it was so. First, he kissed me gently on the cheek.

"The sky is still bright," I offered.

"Do you see the moon?" he asked and he turned me to face the same direction as he.

"Wherever I may be, I will see that same moon, my sweet Pet. We must remember that as long as we gaze upon the same heavenly body, we cannot be far from each other."

He kissed the back of my neck as I caught my breath in a sigh.

"What is it, Lizzie?" he asked.

"It is nothing," I assured him, but continued, "and yet everything." His arms wrapped completely around me and he rotated me to face him.

"Must you go?" I implored. His expression went from sympathetic to joyous.

"Come with me!"

"What?"

"I mean just as far as the train station."

"Cannot you stay one more moment?"

"There, there now. I will inform the conductor that we have not completed our good-byes this evening and surely he will hold the train."

"Oh, you! That is not what I meant." I began walking with him. "It is just that you are always going somewhere. Your journey to Valparaiso is understandable, but must you also go to Weathersfield when you have just returned from Rockwood? I do not want you to love Rockwood more than you love me."

"I could never love anything as much as I love you, my Pet." The lamp behind him caused his eyes to fall into the shadow under his brow. He kissed me again on the mouth and I did not care who might see. The horizon had not yet darkened and I knew there was some risk of being so public with our affections, but I did not know when I might see him again, and I simply did not care what stories one might tell. When he finally pulled away, my heart stopped.

"Good bye, my Pet," he said, and began to step back from me.

"Godspeed, dear Ned," I said and then, "One more thing!" A grin widened across his face. "Another present," I said. "I wanted it to be a surprise, but I cannot wait for you to see it. I am fashioning a ring for you from my hair and have sent it to be finished by Mr. Bowdoin. Do you know the jeweler?"

There was no more delaying the inevitable. The train would wait no longer. As he boarded the train, he kissed his own hand in a most demonstrative manner and threw that kiss for me to catch.

⁕

Saturday, 24 September 1853

By morning there was a chill in the air that threatened an abrupt end to summer. It was not yet light when my feet hit the cold floor searching for my slippers. I scurried about trying not to disturb anyone as I readied to report to Miss Ward's. Father emerged from his room, dressed and ready to greet the sunrise as was his usual discipline. Joe would be rising soon. In Laura's room, she lay with her golden hair completely unraveled from her nightcap and strewn about the side of her bed.

The smell of yeast breads rose from the kitchen. Bridget had the breakfast table set for Father; I joined him as Aunt Eliza queried him about his travel plans.

"Joseph, will you and Joe be heading out today?" she asked.

"We will board at noon and be just two days away. The boy will have to learn to rise with the sun, won't he?"

"God help him," Aunt Eliza placed her palms together and raised her fingertips to her chin.

"What if Joe is disobedient, Father?" I asked. "What will happen to him when he is out at sea?"

"He will learn," was Father's only response.

Aunt Eliza saw my puzzled expression and offered comfort. "You must not worry so about your brother, Lizzie. He will do what he needs to do so as to learn the lessons he has coming. Just keep him in your prayers."

"I will," I said, knowing she meant something more than my typical rote closing to "bless my family. Amen." I vowed to add a little

182

something special for my brother as I was already asking God to watch over my Ned in his travels.

After excusing myself from the table, I hurried to collect my books and be on my way to Miss Ward's.

Children in Miss Ward's School

Methuen Train Depot

CHAPTER 19

Bleak House

Miss M. E. Andrews-
Care of Gen. Joseph Andrews
Salem
Essex Co.
Mass.

Methuen, [Thursday] 29th Sept. 1853

My dear pet-

This is only a missive to say that I am coming, and as I would rather tell you "face to face" everything I have to say, what can I write? I was very near popping down upon you tomorrow instead of Saturday. I had understood your father and Joe were going to St. John on Friday, so I supposed, by forewarning you of my intention today, I could better meet you in the cars tomorrow, than wait till Saturday. Therefore I intended to send you this evening a note by your father; but I found he was not in Boston; and moreover that he was not going to St. John. So don't look for me till Saturday: I will be in the last part of the last car of the one o'clock train. If any of your school-mates are with you, perhaps it will be better for me not to jump out of the car in Salem as I would do.

It makes me feel very lively to think how soon I shall see you and hear you say _________? Oh! pet! Haven't you been tormented dreadfully about the white hat that called at Miss Ward's School last Friday? Ellen Hodges looked at me when she came to the door as if to say 'now I'll plague Lizzie Andrews.' It was a real roguish look.

"I don't want you to love Rockwood better than you love me." Why, my precious darling, how could you think of such a thing? It came out so very cunningly that I was laughing on my way to Boston as I repeated it over to myself. Besides it was new proof how much you loved me, though I didn't need that. You won't be afraid of my loving anything better than you, will you? It is impossible.

There! I have just given your daguerreotype something. Guess what it was? I feel so happy tonight writing to you, with the prospect of meeting you so soon that I can almost fly to Wenham. Don't you wish I could?

The Conductor (last Friday) waited behind me for my ticket very quietly while I was waving to you, and when I turned round (without knowing he was watching) he smiled so funnily that I wanted to laugh out. But I didn't move a feature as I sat down. It was the same Conductor who said I staid a little too long. He came from Salem with us on Friday noon.

I hope Joe will be away by tomorrow with a prospect of beginning to do something. I shall enjoy my short visit much better if I am sure one trouble is removed from you. I suppose Laura received the writing-desk safely on Monday. I have been on the point of telling Mother that I had some presents in Hamilton, but I thought it better to wait. Have you taken the best care of them for me?

In the Mechanics Fair - Boston - I saw a model of the Josephine, and a duplicate of that large daguerreotype of Emily Oliver. I carefully examined S. & H.'s collection to see if he had been honest with me, but I saw nothing like my pet's face. Ellen Hodges is there. Have you been to Mr. Bowdoin's yet?

I have been reading 'Bleak House' for two days. I think you would like it very much. Liz showed me, the other day, in *Godey's* for October an answer to "M. E. A." about patterns for handkerchiefs and asked if that was you. I said 'no.' Was I right? An article in Putnam is attributed to me. I will tell you about it in Hamilton.

I hope my pet will be as happy as possible till Saturday noon, and then I know she will. It is only a few hours till then though it will seem an age. Now - a kiss, dearest - and good-bye for a short time.

Your own Ned-

⁎⟶⟨∞⟩⟵⁎

Tuesday, 4 October 1853

The morning was uneventful, with the exception of an announcement in *the Herald.* Emily Oliver was right; her brother Samuel married Sarah Elizabeth Crosby in Lawrence, Massachusetts yesterday. At Miss Ward's, I received an inquiry from the lovely Ellen Hodges as to the whereabouts of one Mr. Edward Tenney. After informing her he was here recommending Charles Dickens' book *Bleak House,* she took a sudden interest in literature. Not having the book on hand, I challenged her to find a complete copy for the classroom. I advised her the book had been published in twenty weekly installments in *Household Words,* and she could collect and compile the magazine pages, or acquire the book in its entirety. We discussed how she would obtain the story could be at her complete discretion. She beamed, as she returned to her desk.

The next morning, being Saturday, I headed to the Salem library to see if I might procure a copy myself, but left empty-handed. My request would be filled at a future date.

I reached the Salem train station fifteen minutes before the arrival of the one o'clock train. Departures to Wenham were posted, and I confirmed we could depart soon after Edward arrived to meet me at the depot.

Our business in Wenham would take but an hour and we could hop back on the train for the short ride to Hamilton before nightfall. Aunt Eliza expected me to go today, and I saw no reason to inform her that my plans had been arranged based on my cousin's time of arrival in Salem. Of course, if she had asked, I would have told her, though perhaps not mentioned the dreadful excuses I gave my classmates. I told them my preoccupations with family obligations made it necessary for me to travel without their company. After all, Father *had* asked me to stop in Wenham on my way to Hamilton to meet with his customer and make a small delivery.

I checked the small parcel of silks in my bag, tiny remnants that would have little use beyond handkerchiefs. Further examination revealed a variety of plaid patterns, confirming their limited usefulness.

"Does the fabric satisfy your tastes?" a familiar voice asked.

Looking up I responded, "An intriguing pattern for a dress, I might say."

Edward selected a piece, shook it with two hands as if it were sizeable and held it to the light. "A lovely gown," he said with his nose in the air.

"Or a dreadful one," I said. "Have you ever seen a plaid dress?"

He admitted he had not, nor had he noticed their absence when observing recent promenades in New York, but promised to pay better attention.

My cousin was full of news and we enjoyed a pleasant ride to Wenham. Upon our arrival, we walked from the depot through that small town, following the directions Father had provided for accomplishing his errand.

Glancing over my shoulder to read the address, Edward asked, "Do you know who Elizabeth Richards Horton is?"

"I believe she is the daughter of the Richards family who lives in the Claflin-Richards House.”

“Yes, but she also has a home in Boston that is a popular meeting place for neighborhood youngsters. She keeps her childhood toys and dolls there to entertain them. She has so many that she displayed them at a fair to benefit the School for Crippled Children and charged an admission fee of five cents!”

“Is that so?”

“Yes. I saw a posted handbill about the doll exhibit. Lizzie, I heard it was a savvy operation. The exhibit added a full five dollars to the fair proceeds.”

“Do you suppose she would allow us to see them?”

“Do you have a half-dime?”

“I have this!” I held up the parcel. “She wrote Father requesting scraps of silk and he is giving these to her as a donation.” Edward chivalrously relieved me of the parcel. It was the tiniest of burdens but I accepted his offer.

“*We* have this!” he corrected. “Our admission.”

We arrived at the Claflin-Richards House and were graciously welcomed in by Mrs. Horton herself, with no word of a fee. Edward admired the architecture, drawing a comparison to that of the Rockwood Estate, which left Mrs. Horton sufficiently impressed. Her furnishings and decorative artifacts looked to be among the finest in New England and rather unlike others in this small village. Edward guessed that the house was built in 1700 and she appeared quite charmed by his interest.

“1690, to be exact,” she gestured toward us, leading us to the dwelling room.

“This style is reflective of a late 17th century Minister’s parlor with a mid-century bed chamber and a Victorian chamber. Do you see the Ogee braces?” she asked pointing toward the corners of the chamber. “These are typical of 16th and 17th century English dwellings,” she explained with a mix of pride and humility. Her display of toys was sufficient to entertain an entire orphanage for weeks on end.

We left Mrs. Horton's and continued on our way, marveling at how her house contrasted with the small farming town. The wooden sidewalks led to a good number of shoe shops, but we were told we would not find shoe factories nearer than Danvers and Lynn. The primary industry in this village was the harvesting of ice. Wenham Lake ice was known around the world.

Claflin-Richards House in Wenham

There was a small Meeting House that seemed too small for its purpose as a Town Hall. Edward was intrigued by the fire-fighting equipment that adorned its exterior. Ladders, fire hooks and buckets were arranged within easy reach of volunteer fire fighters.

"Perhaps we can find Wenham's own Mr. Bucket."

"Mr. Bucket?" I asked.

"My Pet really must learn about Mr. Bucket, the detective in Scotland Yard portrayed by Mr. Dickens in *Bleak House*. Shall I find you a copy of the book?"

I explained about my pending request and how perhaps Ellen Hodges would find a copy sooner than I might.

"When you read it, you must write and tell me if you think Mrs. Jellyby does not seem to be an apt description of Mrs. Horton. It is said that Mrs. Jellyby pursues distant projects at the expense of her duty to her own family. Although her character has been harshly criticized as being a woman activist like Caroline Chisholm, I think Mrs. Chisholm has done much to help rid English society of its prejudices. Can you imagine the immorality men might fall into, were it not for the love of a fine woman?"

He stopped short in his tracks. "No, you must not even venture to imagine that. Forgive me, my Pet, for letting that slip from my tongue." This, of course, was reason enough for him to sweep his arms around me and place a kiss upon my face.

"Edward!" I scolded, my mock-protest intended to restore our self-respect. He pulled himself into a military stance and saluted, "Yes, ma'am."

"You will be the reason my character follows the highest road. You must demand nothing less of me, my Pet. If anyone can steer me from becoming another Harold Skimpole, it would be you."

"Harold Skimpole? Where does your mind go, Ned?" I asked, thoroughly entertained by his antics.

"To *Bleak House*, my dear. Perhaps I am too much like his character. He is a poet and a critic of literature and theatrical works. Skimpole is much like the poet and essayist James Henry Leigh Hunt. Do you know him?"

"I have heard the name. He is an Englishman, is he not? I cannot recall reading his works, however."

"That matters not. My point is that I surely would fall to such indulgences, having no reason to pursue a proper trade that would allow me to provide for you in the manner to which you are accustomed, if not for my love of you."

"If not for *my* love of *you*." I looked him in the eye and quietly said, "I *do* love you, Ned."

He was speechless for a moment; a rare moment for Edward. My words seemed to hang in the air and echoed through my mind. I think he understood me.

Our conversations were effortless and thereafter constant on our way to Hamilton, despite the occasionally disruptive rattle of the train upon the tracks. We disembarked before dusk. I was ready to retire from so much journeying, regretting not obtaining a new pair of shoes for my weary feet.

The house where I boarded was not far from the train station. My cousin was to stay the night also and I knew we must be beyond reproach in our mannerisms.

"I must call you *cousin* now, or I will call you Mr. Tenney, maybe *Edward*, nothing too familiar. The walls have ears."

"Oh yes, and a small town like Hamilton has ample noses willing to poke themselves into our business, which is none of theirs." Edward hunched over and began to sniff at the air like a melodramatic actor portraying an investigator. Affecting a strange accent, he continued, "Tongues would wag all the way back to Salem, if anyone caught wind of this scandal, ma'dam."

He held the door for me, as I entered to greet the Goody, a woman whose name I struggled to recall, although she had been working at the boarding house for some time. "Hello, this is my cousin, Mr. Edward Tenney.

"Of course, Lizzie. Your cousin Mr. Edward Tenney may stay in the back room," she repeated my full description for Edward, and handed him the key, directing him to his room. I heard her ask him, "Have you a bag?"

"I carry what I need in my coat, thank you." Edward said, and patted his breast pocket as he threw me a smile.

"Call on me when you are ready to meet for supper," I said.

"Yes, ma'am," he responded as he rounded the corner.

The evening was short, but pleasant enough to ensure a long rest.

In the morning, I showed him around Hamilton. We talked

discreetly about what it might be like to live in such a town as a married couple. His dreams made my head heavy with desire and upon retiring my poor feather pillow could hardly support me satisfactorily. Although in my usual bed, nothing felt familiar. I longed for the night when I would rest my head on his shoulder and be comforted in his arms.

Several times during the night, I awoke with a start, thinking he had entered my room and whispered something to me, but 'twas only a dream. The next morning as we breakfasted and strolled through Hamilton, he told me of his night and dreams that he was in my bed holding me in his arms. I think we might have had the same dream.

By late morning we headed back to Salem to meet Grandmother for our mid-day dinner. The family greeted us without too much gossip about where we had been, though we heard Aunt Gray ask Grandmother if Edward planned to live in Hamilton, and why she hadn't been invited to our wedding. Our poor old Aunt seemed confused to hear there had been no announcement about any engagement.

After much discussion about our obligations and schedules, we accepted an invitation for tea at Grandmother's on Tuesday. I would be leaving for Hamilton and Edward delighted at the excuse to return to Salem. He insisted he escort me home before returning to Methuen, so we took our leave. His company was in much demand these days. Though his departure date remained uncertain, all the family wished to visit and bid him bon voyage. My sister was no different. As we approached the house, Laura burst from the front door, her arms outstretched.

"Thank you, cousin, my most dearly beloved cousin. I have already written to you twice and hope my letter will be the first you receive in Valparaiso!"

"So, you received the writing desk?" Edward asked, nodding at me.

"Yes, it is heavenly! Here is the very first I have written with it." She displayed a neatly folded envelope inscribed *My dearest cousin Edward.* The back hosted an abundance of sealing wax impressed with a scroll-ing *L.*

"Thank you," he said.

"Thank YOU!" She flung her arms around him and kissed him on his cheek, twice.

"I wish I had a brother like *you*." Pulling back, her expression was distressed. She added, "But, I am certain that would not suit my sister one bit, so you must remain my cousin. Do come in." She put her arm in his and the three of us jostled ourselves onto the front steps.

Aunt Gray was at tea, which is the most either of us had seen her in many years. Edward was the only gentleman among numerous aunts and matrons, but he was perfectly comfortable entertaining them with his stories.

Saying good-bye, he promised a letter by week's end and faithful to his word, it arrived on Friday. I devoured it on my way to Miss Ward's, disappointed at some of its news. I simply was not fit for sharing him so freely.

Men's white hats

CHAPTER 20

The White Hat

Miss M. E. Andrews
Care of Gen. J. Andrews
Salem
Mass.

Wednesday A. M. 5th Oct. /53
[postmarked Methuen]

Dear Pet,

I feel so lonesome without you that I can't resist this opportunity of having a little chat with you, but, as I must leave some room for Friday's letter, I will limit myself to half a sheet. Didn't you miss me at the depot yesterday noon when you went to Hamilton? I was tempted to call for you at school to say 'Good-bye' before I took the cars, but I thought what Ellen Hodges would say if she recognized the white hat so soon again. How I wish my precious little pet would come and lay her head on my shoulder now. Won't she! She would if she could?

Mrs. Osgood & Mary and Mrs. Carlton had some gentle hints about my going to Hamilton and I laughed in my sleeve. Lucy O. was at Dr. Fisk's. I met Mrs. Sprague & Harriet. Mrs. S. was going to Boston and H. would say nothing but Rockwood.

She asked lots of questions; I could only say "Yes marm" or "No marm." She began to give me some good advice, but just then I had to go away. I was very sorry to leave her, of course. Now Ned, you must not tell "stories." Please excuse me won't you? - But you know some folks are very tedious and H. S. is one of that sort.

I displayed my presents as soon as I reached home last evening. "Whose are those," said Margie. "How beautiful!" "Why Edward!" etc. etc. Liz says she must finish hers immediately so that I won't wear yours out. I am going to put the nice ones on only upon extra occasions and Sundays. Oh! I am so very much obliged to you "Dear pet!" – "Dear Ned" How cunning! I wish that imagining you nestling upon my shoulder would only bring you there.

Don't forget to send in your letter what you promised. Don't forget Mr. Bowdoin. Don't forget Ned. How cruel it was for me to say that last, wasn't it? Will you forgive me, dearest? May I kiss you just once? I feel so funny away from you that I don't know how to write. It seems as if I would give the world to see you now. Write me what was happening to you today (Wednesday) between eleven and one -(forenoon). I wonder if there is not some electric communication at work between us. It seems as if you wanted me very much at just this time. I have a presentiment that you are exposed to some danger, and need me to defend you. "Good-bye"

Thursday 6th Oct. Such a fright as I had last night, my darling! When I went at night to bid my pet 'Good-night,' I could not find my key. In the same drawer with the daguerreotype was this letter, and I was afraid both might be seen. I hunted all over the house but the missing key was not to be seen, and I went to bed without seeing you. This, added to the feeling I had had that you were "in danger," made me so nervous that it was a long time before I could fall asleep. But this morning as soon as I was up I found the key below. Didn't I rush up to my room and seize my darling as if I were never to let her go again? It seemed such a relief to see you once more. Think how I should feel to go away without any likeness of you.

When I reached Methuen on Tuesday I found a letter from Chas. Jarvis telling me to fulfill my promise of visiting Vermont. I did not care to go now, it is so late, but as they have sent I shall go up for a few days on Friday. I shall probably spend a week there; so please direct Sunday's letter to me at Weathersfield - Vt. The Post-office is near by Mr. Jarvis', and that they may not take out your letter, please direct in care of "Alfred S. Clinton, Weathersfield, Vt." Next Friday, as the mail from W. may reach Boston earlier than the Methuen mail you had better call for my letter when you go in to school, though it may not come till later.

Dear Lizzie, as the time draws near for me to leave New England, I think more and more every day of our separation. I shall probably not go before November, but it is only three weeks till then. We must not neglect any opportunity of meeting in the meanwhile. For though I could only see you for a few moments yet that would be something to think of when we are so far apart. If you can come to Boston for a day, it would be so pleasant for us both. Perhaps it may be more convenient for you to be in Boston next week. If so, send to me at W. (allowing two days or three if possible for me to receive your letter) and come to Boston. I wish I wasn't going to Vt. but it is too late now, for C. Jarvis is to meet me on Friday. Though I might enjoy myself any other time, yet now I want to spend every moment I can find with you.

I have just read what I have written & I hope you won't think I write foolishly, will you? You know I always want to write to you as I would talk, and I have almost imagined your head nestling on my shoulder while I have been writing. Oh! if I could only be with you every day till I sail I should be so happy.

If I don't see your father in Boston, will you say something to him about my coming to Wenham again! Last Tuesday I was so nervous in Salem for fear that we might meet your father that I could hardly keep quiet. If he had seen us in Essex St. or Grandmother's, he would have been so much provoked that I should hardly have dared come again. Wasn't Aunt Gray's remark rather funny. She thinks we are engaged.

I am going to send something in this letter. Please tell me if you receive it safely?

Perhaps we can arrange some plan by which I may ride out in the cars with you from Salem without any one knowing it, can't we?

Tonight I am going to see some tableaux at Mrs. Green's with Liz and Mary. Don't you wish we could spend the evening together? I think of nothing but you now, the whole time. Tomorrow morning I leave for Vermont.

I must stop somewhere, though I keep thinking of something left unsaid. Remember my "nom du plume" for Weathersfield? Good bye, my dear Lizzie, till I can write again, I send you something else, dearest, but you can't see it.

Your own Ned.

I hope you will have to consult Dr. Minifield in Boston soon. Do let your feet trouble you a little if you can.

I am going to dream about you tonight, I know it will be so pleasant.

Good bye

I am afraid you will never find an end to this letter, but I have no more room.

I must add the last word. I saw a lady in a plaid silk dress in Boston so you can go to Mr. B's in what you think most becoming to you. I shall expect such a nice long letter from you next Tuesday. I don't think there will be any objection to my spending some afternoon at Hamilton soon, will there? If Laura would not tell of it.

Good bye - dearest.
Don't you want to see Ned?

⎯⎯⎯⎯⎯ ⎯⎯⎯⎯⎯

Saturday, 8 October 1853

My poor sweet Ned, surrounded by the widow Mrs. Osgood and Mrs. Carlton, both of whom wish to insert themselves into his personal business, and to mine. Aunts so often do that and I expect they insist it is their prerogative. In addition, Ned has the company of his spinster cousin Mary Osgood to contend with! Shame on me! I should not call her such, as she is but his age, and truly sweet and kind. One simply imagines her devotion to her mother might lead her to remain unmarried.

Then, to encounter Lucy Osgood, oh dear, how will we ever retain our privacy and protect our secret engagement with so many extended family members watching him at every step of his journey through life. Fortunately, Mrs. Sprague and Cousin Harriet had insufficient time to become a problem, as they are thankfully more interested in the mansion Rockwood! He truly is safer to spend his time with his sisters and neighbors listening to their stories and admiring their pictures.

As these thoughts tumbled through my head, I looked around to ensure no family member of mine was nearby. I shifted my position to release one of my skirt stays from pinching my ribs. Bridget's vigor with my corset laces this morning left little room for expressions of awe or woe. I sat on a bench near the post office, Ned's letter in hand, catching my breath. When the pounding in my heart subsided, I continued walking and reading…and thinking…What if some danger so afflicted me that I never saw Edward again?

He is only two days distance from me, I reasoned. That distance could keep him from me for far too long, if something were to happen. You must not think so, I scolded myself. My feelings spoke louder than my reasoning. Soon, months and years would come between us. How will we bear such separation?

Childish impatience pierced my confidence, and I struggled to push my fear from my mind. I folded Edward's letter neatly, tucking it in my bag. I need to compose myself sufficiently to prepare to fulfill a full week of my duties at Miss Ward's. I took a breath and looked up. I could see Aunt Eliza outside in her garden. She loves to put her garden to bed for the winter. I could see her tucking plants under fallen leaves and spreading straw around as if it were a luxurious winter blanket. I joined her. Not moments later, I realized my angst had been buried along with any trace of fear about my future.

At week's end, students bustled out the door to embrace the weekend with their usual enthusiasm. My own excitement was nowhere to be found. I stepped from Miss Ward's, feeling so much heaviness I feared I might plummet through the stair. I could see Father walking inside our house, his paper and pipe in hand. By the time I entered, he was in his office with his face hidden by the newspaper. He heard me, and he greeted me. I sank into a nearby chair, hugging my shawl around my shoulders.

"What is it, Lizzie?" he asked.

My mouth drew tight. Tears began to trickle from my eyes.

"I am trying to be strong, Father."

"Strong?" He put down his paper and set his pipe on a nearby table.

"I am eighteen years of age, and yet I feel like such a child. I'm so unprepared to live on my own."

"Are you planning to leave us, my dear?"

"Well, no."

"Good. We would miss you."

"I will go away someday."

"I expect you will."

"It is just that I do not know where I will go."

"Is that something you need to decide now?"

"No, not exactly."

"Lizzie, do you even know what is troubling you? Did something happen today at Miss Ward's?"

"No, school was fine." The tears welled up again.

"Then what is it?" he asked, seeming impatient.

"I received a letter from Edward this morning."

"Is there a problem?" He looked concerned, and I felt how woefully inadequate my communication was.

"He is in Weathersfield, Vermont. Charles Jarvis insisted he visit." I hesitated. Father's curious expression showed evidence he did not understand my problem. I continued, "I miss him dreadfully."

"Now I see what this is all about," Father was smiling now.

"Why do you smile? Am I so amusing?"

"No, no, but you are young and, at times, silly." He then asked, "How long is Edward expected to be away?"

"He will be gone a week."

"And when he returns, will you see him before he departs for Valparaiso?"

"I cannot be sure, Father. I may never see him again."

"Now, Lizzie, is that likely?" Father was beginning to lose his patience with me.

"Well, no," I admitted. "He would be here now, but for his kind regard of Charles Jarvis. He wishes he were here. Father, he is to be away for three years! Once he is gone, I will simply die."

"Lizzie, your life will continue, and Edward will make a proper good-bye before his departure, if he possibly can. I expect that is what he is doing in Weathersfield—making a proper good-bye. The Jarvises are his family as much as we are, my dear. We must not be selfish."

"Am I dreadfully selfish?"

"Not dreadfully. The Honorable Judge Jarvis is a very important man. He can be extremely helpful to Edward, like a father."

"He is not visiting his uncle, rather his cousin!" I protested.

"A cousin," he said with great deliberation, "like you." Father continued. "Dear child, can you not see how his family yearns for his company? Perhaps you could feel some happiness that he is so loved."

"I will try," I said, standing up, hoping to end the conversation. "You are right," I continued, placing my hand lightly on his shoulder. "I shall not embarrass myself any further with my self-pity. Thank you, Father," I said and removed myself from his office and headed upstairs to my room.

I intended to compose my response to Edward's letter. Arranging my pen and stationery, I positioned myself at my writing table with just enough afternoon light to see. My hand was not producing words. I forced myself to write, "Dear Mr. Clinton." Thoughts of what I might say to someone with such a name simply evaded me. Soon, the sun began casting long shadows over my letter. A chill came over me, just as Bridget appeared to call us to supper.

⁓

Father brought me a new letter on Friday, which I accepted, knowing several blank sheets lay in my bedroom drawer unfinished. The only one I sent must have been dreadfully delayed. My family had become accustomed to seeing me retire to the parlor on a Friday afternoon to read. Laura would arrive at dusk from Hamilton and settle in to reading her latest *Godey's*. On occasion, Aunt Eliza would join us with her handiwork or a book. More often, she occupied herself in the garden or offered her assistance at Grandmother's or to charitable undertakings in the neighborhood. Once again, Father and I fell company to each other and I realized my good fortune in having him as my confidante.

⁓

CHAPTER 21

Mr. Clinton

Brig. Genl. Andrews
Salem
Mass
For Miss M. E. Andrews

Weathersfield, Vt. [Wednesday] 12th Oct. 1853

Dear Pet

I was quite disturbed by the non-reception of your letter on Monday or Tuesday, particularly as I have had to watch the mail every day lest Kate Jarvis should take out the letter. But today (Wednesday) as I sat in the Post-office, which is the kitchen of a neighboring house, the Post-mistress handed Mr. Clinton your letter. As the letters are not advertised I had to ask for "Mr. Clinton" last Monday.

I am writing in my room tonight, with a poor light and bad pen. So you must excuse the looks of my letter. Weathersfield is a very pleasant place to visit, but I should enjoy myself much more, if I did not have in view the separation from you and the desire to spend all the time I can with you. I shall be at Methuen before next Tuesday morning so please direct to Ned as usual.

If you go to Boston next week Wednesday or Thursday (or later) be sure and appoint the time and place as I should not have time to write before seeing you. I have wished every night that you could be here to bid me "good-night." Your name has been mentioned every day by some of the Jarvises in connection with mine. I said once "Oh, Lizzie & I are the best friends in the world," though probably my real meaning was not understood.

I did not reach Weathersfield till Saturday, as I had to stop over night at White River. They have plenty of horses and I have been on horse-back one half of the time. Once I rode with Kate. Charles is a very pleasant fellow, and I spend a large part of the time out of doors with him. There is an old maid aunt and a little girl with whom I talk evenings. Mr. Jarvis is very pleasant and entertaining. I know all the neighbors very well. Kate and Louisa say that I am captivated with Miss Danvorth, the Post-mistress, because I hurry over there every night as soon as the mail is in sight. Don't be jealous -- She is almost 40 years old. Perhaps you can guess the true reason of my being so anxious about the mail. The P. Mistress thinks my name is Clinton and I was afraid she would send my letter over with the Jarvis bundle.

Didn't I choose a romantic name? Oh! Pet! I have just thought there are no envelopes so that I can't write on the last page. There was everything I had to say. Do come to Boston if you can. If any one accompanies you from Salem perhaps Mrs. Haven's will be a good place to meet. Thursday will be the best day for your letter may miss one mail. Think how far we are from each other now; how far we may be in a month. I think there is no probability of my sailing before November, though I have not heard from Uncle Edwin. I have had a glimpse of you every night but that doesn't satisfy me. But I hope to see you soon. Till I do my darling

"Good-bye"
Ned

You will excuse the appearance of this letter won't you for I have been writing with a dreadful light.

Good night dear pet.

I expect to see Edward Cutts tomorrow. He is going away from home and is in love *again*.

⁕

Saturday, 15 October 1853

Remaining busy during the past week tempered my despair at my Ned venturing so far away. I thought he might dismiss me as rude and inconsiderate when my letter failed to arrive as scheduled. My remorse was even greater, however, when I learned he wrote in near darkness, while I handily set aside my sheet at the casting of a mere shadow. While I am comfortably surrounded by family and neighbors, never far from class-mates, he spends evenings with an old maid and a little girl. Yet, his spirit remains strong; while I struggle to keep my spirits up. As I enjoyed familiar surroundings in the company of my family, he is a guest in a dark house, conversing with people he does not know well.

"That would be just like Edward," I thought out loud, yearning for his attention.

"I beg your pardon?" Father glanced at me briefly. He sat as he usually does in the evening, paper in hand and pipe tamped with fresh tobacco.

"Father?" I asked, bewildered, in response to his question, for truly I did not realize words had left my lips within range of his hearing.

"You said, 'That would be just like Edward'," he said and waited, clearly seeking an explanation.

"Well," I paused. "Edward is visiting other people besides Charles at the Jarvis' home, including an old maid and a little girl. It seems kind of him and… just like him."

Father gazed out the window toward the street, seeming to focus on nothing. Finally he said, "The little girl is probably the daughter of

205

Charles' older sister, Elizabeth, who died five years ago. The mother-in-law cares for the child now."

"Oh." How could I feel jealous of a little girl who had lost her mother? I had felt that myself; so had Edward. Father's distant expression made me think he was missing my mother now. He once admitted he missed her every day. I could not imagine bearing such loss daily for 12 years.

Father told me we must honor the dead, but turn our thoughts to the living, if we are to carry on.

"Kate and Louisa are there also, Father." I offered.

"They are Charles' younger sisters," Father said. I nodded in silence and Father returned to his paper.

Reluctant to intrude into his evening ritual, I simply watch him. He is a tall man, commanding. His angular jaw defines a long, narrow face with a straight but somewhat prominent nose. He never seems hurried or burdened. He goes about his business plainly, keeping track of his family, neighbors, brethren and beyond. Not only does he assist those in Salem, but also in Boston. He recently paid for a shipment of goods from the Orient after learning another merchant was unable to secure necessary funds in time to accept delivery. Father sold some goods, but provided the bulk of his acquisition to the original merchant once he was able to pay. When I asked him about it, he modestly said it worked out fine for everyone.

"Father?" I interrupted my own thoughts before I knew what I was about to ask.

"Yes?" He looked at me with an expression of anticipation.

"May I bring another parcel of silk remnants to Wenham, so I might accept an invitation to tea with Mrs. Horton?" I asked. "She has the most marvelous doll collection with fashions one might see in Boston or New York, nothing out of season."

"You have already delivered what I had. Perhaps you should call on your Aunt Dolly. She might provide hat-making materials that would delight Mrs. Horton."

"What a splendid idea, Father." I was determined to call on Aunt Dolly before responding to Edward's letter. Perhaps, I could arrange my next meeting with Edward in Wenham. Wenham is closer for me than Boston, and I would be less likely to encounter unexpected acquaintances. Considering the distance Edward would have traveled, Mrs. Horton would be certain to extend an invitation for hospitality overnight. Such a meeting would be a perfect collusion.

I prepared a note for Mrs. Horton advising her to expect another delivery. Then I wrote Edward of my plans, which I was certain, would be confirmed by Aunt Dolly in the early morning. I posted both letters promptly thereafter. My own cunning lifted my spirits. I was no longer at the mercy of the postmaster's delivery schedule or Edward's ability to pen a new letter. I had taken charge of my destiny and was preparing to make it sparkle, like the brightest star in the New England skies.

The End
(or the beginning of a wonderful life)

Continue reading to enjoy a preview of...

Will You Wait For Me?
Book Three
The Courtship of Lizzie Andrews

Edward Tenney has graduated from Harvard and is preparing to ship out to make his fortune, at which time he aspires to make a public announcement of his engagement to Lizzie Andrews. When his father's death put him as the head of his household, he embraced the responsibility to support his step-mother and five siblings. While obtaining business education experience in Boston and New York, he continues to enjoy the entertainments of the time, social visits with prominent persons, and an occasional rendezvous with his betrothed. He secures a position as a clerk on a new steamer headed to Valparaiso, Chile and anticipates a three-year absence before he returns. Book Three begins with a quick and urgent note from Edward's to Lizzie to arrange a rendevous.

CHAPTER 1

Wenham

Miss M. E. Andrews
Care Gen. Andrews
Salem
Mass.

Miss Andrews
at Miss Ward's School
Salem
Mass.

Wednesday, 2d Nov./ 53

Dear L.

I am going to dine with Liz at Lynn today and in the afternoon
will ride out to Wenham and pass the night, if convenient to you.
I shall probably take the train which leaves Boston at 4 P.M. but
possibly earlier -

G.B.
E.

I arrived in Wenham just past three, clutching Edward's note, and spotted a white hat on the platform. Could it be Edward arrived earlier than anticipated? My bulky parcel of millinery pieces at my side, the white hat surfaced from a sea of black and swept us both along with the waves of passengers exiting the depot.

"Aunt Dolly is my favorite," the charmed one in the white hat said, more funnily than anything I had heard before. He pulled me gently, but determinedly, onto a bench just outside the station.

"I just want to look at you, Lizzie," he said. "I want to flood my eyes with your likeness until my head is full." A woman walked past and stopped in front of us, seeming to look for someone.

Edward fell silent, and then ventured into conversation fitting for public consumption.

"What have you brought for Mrs. Horton?" he asked.

I opened my parcel and began nervously displaying its contents, knowing the show was a diversion.

"What do you think of this veil for a hat?" I asked and held it in front of my face. Edward placed a hand on each of mine, looking to assure the woman overhearing us had politely turned away. He caressed the veil across my face holding my cheeks gently in his palms.

"Aunt Dolly said this miniature hat sample would be perfect for a doll," I explained, as if he held an interest in dolls. I tried to move my face as little as possible from the warm caress of his hands. "Since she no longer needs this particular hat style, she provided it for our project."

He leaned forward, as if to examine the details in my veil. "You look like a gypsy, my pet," he whispered closely in my ear.

A man approached the woman bystander, remarked about finding someone to fetch their luggage, and they hurried off, paying us no attention.

"A gypsy?" I implored a bit too loudly. "I only see one gypsy on this bench." I rose abruptly and proceeded to walk away. Edward scrambled to replace the items in my parcel, and appeared swiftly at my side, laughing.

"You cannot escape my affections as easily as that!" he scolded and presented the crook of his elbow to escort me.

"Thank God," I responded and threaded my hand though the opening, which he quickly pressed close to his side.

We meandered toward the Claflin-Richards House on Main Street languishing in each other's company, knowing we would be unfashionable to arrive early. We paused to look at shoes in the shops. I prodded Edward to describe for me what he might select for his fiancé, and we enjoyed our silly conversation.

By the time we reached Mrs. Horton's we had arranged our next rendezvous—Edward would arrive in Salem by train on Saturday in time to meet Nellie Abbot, my companion for tea. I would act surprised, as if this were an accidental meeting, and casually invite Edward to join us.

"What shall I say?" I asked Edward, "Shall I say, 'oh my, what a surprise, my beloved secret fiancé has miraculously arrived at this very moment! I do hope he is available to stay for tea?'"

"Now, Lizzie," Edward scolded. "You know I am thinking only of your reputation, my darling. We must avert any scandal that could arise, as many are too easily tempted to gossip. Can you act as if you did not expect me?"

"Of course I can. I am a supreme actor, for I just now convinced you that I might be fool enough to expose our tryst."

"You are a naughty gypsy, my pet, but you are my own and I would like to take you in my arms this very moment and taste a bite of that salty lie that just left your tongue." He said, in a low, matter-of-fact tone, so passersby could not ascertain the spicy words his mouth emitted.

"Edward! You are making it very difficult for me to maintain the very reputation that you so promise to protect."

To be continued...

About the Authors

PJ Watters

Elisabeth C. Johnson

PJ studied writing, theater, filmmaking and dance before earning her B.A. in Art. After writing poetry and a biography of her father, she earned a Master's degree in Health Science and Health Education and worked for two decades as a healthcare executive. Her circuitous professional path led her to become a professional fundraiser. She resides in Spokane, Washington with George Watters, her husband for more than three decades.

Elisabeth earned her B.A. in Art and worked in New York for Carnegie Endowment for International Peace. After marrying A. Albert Johnson and having four daughters, she was widowed at age 35. She moved to California to teach art, later launching a craft business designing stuffed animals and ceramic Pot Pets. An avid genealogist, she researched people in Edward's letters for ten years. She resides with her dog Koko in Washington, Utah and more than sixty gold medals she won for Senior Games archery.